Gildoran went off in the direction he had last seen the Captain moving, toward the cliff lined with tall bushes and their green cup-shaped blossoms.

He felt a strange unease that was almost tangible. After he had walked a few hundred feet along the cliff, his unease turned to real worry; Gilhart should have known better than to wander off alone on a planet that hadn't been completely checked out.

Then Gildoran saw something from the corner of his eye—a square of bluish-white, too regular to be a natural object in all this green. He pushed the branches aside, and found Gilhart crumpled in a heap.

Angry and apprehensive, Gildoran bent over him, unfastening his tunic and anxiously hunting for a pulse. But he already knew that the Captain was dead.

ENDLESS
VOYAGE

by
Marion Zimmer Bradley

ace books
A Division of Charter Communications Inc.
1120 Avenue of the Americas
New York, N.Y. 10036

ENDLESS VOYAGE

An Ace Book

" 'Tis not too late to seek a better world."
Tennyson

Part One

PLANETS ARE FOR SAYING GOODBYE

I

Planets are for saying goodbye.

That's an old saying in the Explorers. I never believed it before. It never really hit me.

Never again. You never really realize what never means. It's a word you use all the time, but it means . . . it means never. NEVER. Not in all the millions of billions of trillions of it. . . .

Get hold of yourself, dammit!

Everything on this planet had changed, but not the pattern of the Explorer Ship: it was lighted now from inside, and outlined in silver; a chained Titan, shadowed against the dark mass of the mountain that rose behind the new city.

The city was still raw, a mass of beams and scars in the wounded red clay of the planet's surface. Gildoran had first seen the great ship outlined against the mountain two years ago, planetside time—before the city had risen there, before *anything* had risen there—and every day since, but now it felt as if he hadn't ever seen it before. There were strange sharp edges on everything, as if the air had dissolved and he saw them hard-edged in space.

Never again. I was a fool to think anything could be different.

How could Janni have done this to me?

I thought she was different. Every fool kid thinks that about the first woman he cares about.

Gildoran passed through the gates. They were still guarded, but that was only a formality. On every planet Gildoran had known—he could remember four in twenty-two years of biological time—the earthworms kept away from Explorer ships.

I took Janni. I thought she'd have to feel the way I did. Wonder, and awe. But she was bored. I should have known then, but instead I was flattered, I thought it was just that she'd rather be alone with me. Maybe she would. Then.

That seems a long time ago now.

The guard didn't bother checking the offered ident disk. It was a formality anyhow. Gildoran's identity was on his face, like all Explorers. He knew what was whispered about them, but lifelong training made it beneath Gildoran's dignity to notice it or seem to remember it.

But I remember. Keep away, they say. Keep away from the Explorers. Keep your children away. They'll steal your children, steal your women.

I wouldn't have stolen Janni. But I might have stayed with her.

He walked with the arrogant pride of all the Explorers, conscious, and proud, of the differences that set him off—set him off cruelly, a planetman might have said—from the rest of the swarming humanity around the city, the crews working to load the ships. He stood seven feet seven, although he was tall even for an Explorer, due to a childhood and youth spent at minimal gravity. The white—paper-white—skin and bleached white hair were colorless from years of hard radiation. He knew there were other differences, bone-deep, marrow-deep, cell-deep. Gene-deep. He never thought about them. But he had known from childhood that no one else ever forgot them.

Janni hadn't forgotten them.
Not for a moment.

The crews around the ship parted to let him through, edging faintly back as he passed. But this was at the edge of his consciousness. He would only have noticed it if they hadn't.

Had she only wanted an exotic? Was it only his strangeness that had attracted her? Not romance, but a perverse desire for the bizarre, the alien, the freakish?
Did women like Janni boast of an Explorer lover, as they might boast the romantic conquest of a gladiator from Vega 16?

Gildoran, feeling faintly sick, moved toward the refuge of the ship.

It's beautiful, more beautiful than anything else they'll ever build here. But it doesn't belong, and neither do I, and now I know it.

Behind him the new city was swarming with life, multiplex human, parahuman and nonhuman life, the life of a Galaxy which had achieved the Transmitter and was no longer limited anywhere by space or time. Life showed all sizes, shapes, colors and integuments. Isolation and differences had vanished. All through history, from the first stirrings of consciousness in man and nonman, transportation—of people, of goods and services and ideas—had been the one bottleneck jamming mankind to an even rate of growth. But with the advent of the Transmitter, consciousness in the Galaxy had outstripped that limitation, and now there were no such limitations.

Or only one limitation. The speed of the Explorers.
Without us, none of this would be here.
But we're still the freaks. We live in time and distance. They live free of them.
But only because of us.

The hint of a new planet to be opened, a new world to be developed and explored, the creation of new labor markets, new projects and products, new work of every kind from running ditch-digging machines to selling women for use and pleasure, had brought them swarming here from the first minute the Transmitter booths had been hooked into the Galactic network. Right here in the city behind him there were big red men from Antares and small bluish men from Aldebaran, furred men from Corona Borealis Six and scaly men from Vega 14, and there were women to match all of them and more.

8

Every new, just-opened world was like this. A carnival of new life for the young, of second—or third, or twenty-third—chances for the old; for the misfits, the excitement-seekers, the successes wanting new worlds to conquer and the failures who hadn't lost hope that *this* time they'd make it big.

But Gildoran walked through it, indifferent. He didn't bother looking back at the city.

There's nothing there for me now. There never was. Only Janni, and I know now she was never really there. Not for me.

He had no part in this world anymore. Once the Transmitter was set up on any world, the Explorers were finished with it. The Explorer ship which had found the world, explored it, subdued it sufficiently to build a Transmitter there, officially opened it, had nothing left to do. Nothing, that is, except to collect their tremendous fee from Head Centre, and lift off to find another one. The *Gypsy Moth* had been here for a year and a half. It was time to move on.

There are other worlds out there, waiting. Plenty of them.

Yes, damn it, and women on all of them.

Someone called Gildoran by name and he looked round, seeing over the heads of the crowd the white, bleached hair and starred tiaras of two of his companions from the *Gypsy Moth*. He slackened pace to let them catch up with him.

Raban was twice Gildoran's age, a man in his forties—biological time, of course, although he had probably been born several hundred years before by sidereal or objective reckoning—with the small stars on his sleeve that meant officialdom on the ship. Ramie was a small fair girl whose great dark eyes showed that she had belonged to one of the pigmented races before the ship radiation got in its work. Now her skin and hair were lucent pale like Gildoran's own, but the eyes retained a long, curious tilt, and her voice had a light and fluting quality.

"It won't be long now, will it?"

"About midnight," Raban said. "Sorry to leave?"

Sorry, oh God, a wrench like death, never again, never again. . . . oh, Janni, Janni, Janni . . .

Gildoran made himself grin, although it felt stiff. "You must be kidding. It was a beautiful planet, but look what they've done to it." He gestured toward the noise, and construction scars behind them. "Like a big nasty mushroom growing up overnight."

Ramie waved at the night sky behind her. Beyond the blurring of the first vapor lights, coming on in the growing sunset, a few pale stars were visible behind the mountain.

"There are lots of other worlds out there. One thing the Universe never runs short of is planets." She smiled shyly at Gildoran, "Why aren't you at the Ceremonial Leavetaking?"

"Why aren't *you?*" They all laughed. Raban said gravely, "I've been thanking all the Gods I ever heard of, as well as a few I made up for the occasion, that I'm still important enough to duck such occasions."

"I almost went," Ramie said. "After all, this world has been home to me for a couple of years. I grew up here, really. It ought to mean *something* to me, even if I'm not sure *what*. And there's something funny about realizing that we'll never see it again—or at least anyone we've ever known on it . . . that even if we spent six months or less in space, and landed on another world with a Transmitter, and came back, it would be fifty or sixty years later planetside, and the girls I played with would be grandmothers."

Never again. . . .

Gildoran said, low, "I know. It hit me, too."

Raban said "Planets are for leaving. For an Explorer, anyhow. After a while—" Gildoran sensed that he meant to comfort them, somehow, even though his voice was hard and unemotional, "you get so they all look the same to you."

They fell silent, crossing the great, grassy, undeveloped expanse at the foot of the mountain, toward the ships, and Gildoran thought about planets. Before this one, they *had* all been the same, so maybe they would again. He'd known four. Not counting, of course, the world where he'd been born, though he didn't remember that one. He knew where it was, of course, as everyone seemed to *know*, although it was bad form to let anyone know that you knew. When you were an Explorer, your home world was your Ship, and the planet where you had actually been birthed, or decanted, or cultured, or hatched, was something you were expected to forget.

He was Gildoran, and his world was the *Gypsy Moth.* And that was all he was. Forever. His official legal ident was G-M Gildoran, just as Raban was G-M Gilraban, and Ramie was G-M Gilramie, and his only compatriots were those bearing the G-M Gil- prefix to their names.

Because you had no other world. You could never go back to any planet, once you left it; the inexorable march of time and slippage outside the sun-systems meant that once you lifted your Ship from any planet you had ever visited, it would be generations further on, unrecognizable, by the time you landed and could visit it again.

While you were living on a planet, of course, you were free of the inexorable drag of time. You could be here today and on Vega 19 tomorrow and three hours later step into a Transmitter booth and be back here again, or on Aldebaran or Antares, and only three hours would have elapsed. (Oh, technically there was a three-quarter of a second lapse inside the booth. It had something to do with Galactic Drag.) But outside the planetary magnetic fields, the freedom from time, the simultaneous transit all over the Galaxy, was gone. You spent six weeks, six months, a year in space, aging only by your biological clock inside. Your cells aged six months, a year. But the Galaxy went on without you; all the network of planets linked by Transmitter went on slipping past, and when you landed on a planet again, by sidereal time it was eighty or a hundred years later.

So when you left, when you said goodbye to a planet it was always forever. And the new worlds might be beautiful, or terrible, but they were always new and strange; and the old worlds, if you faced the shock and went back to them, were new and strange too. You were immortal, as far as the Galaxy was concerned, but you were always shaken loose from what you had known before. . . .

Gildoran turned to Raban and asked suddenly "Is it always like this? Is every new world spoiled—*every* time? Are we always just finding new worlds for people to come in and wreck them, and use them up?"

Raban laughed, but the younger two could see how grave his eyes were. He said, "Remember, they don't think of it as spoiling, but developing; civilizing. Most people like their worlds built up a little. Don't judge them."

He shook his feet fastidiously free of the mud at the base of the great ship, and said, laughing, "Maybe civilization isn't so bad. I've often wondered why we don't have them pave the approaches to the ship. After all, we've had to use this walkway for two years now, and I've wrecked my footgear every time!"

He pointed. "Look, the service men are clearing away the scaffolding. We'll probably be cleared by midnight. I know everyone was supposed to check in by Tenth Hour. Now they'll probably have a stack of last-minute errands for everybody."

He swung up the steps; Gildoran and Ramie followed more slowly, turning to look down at the workmen loading materials and provisions through the lower hatchways. Small shacks, recreation units, all were being taken down and rolled away on enormous trundling cranes and machinery. Eventually the steps themselves would go.

The girl at his side, Gildoran climbed the steps and passed into the familiar, pale-gilded, cool-lighted halls of the lower levels. They were both silent as they went along the lower corridors, stepped into a gravity-shaft and rose upward to the living levels. Raban had dropped off somewhere below, on business of his own; the younger two did not really miss him. He was older and, at least technically, still in authority over them, so that they felt freer when he had gone. But they didn't talk. Gildoran was lost in wrenching regrets and memories, and the girl was silent too.

I wonder if everyone has something they can't bear to leave, and knows they must?

Ramie had friends here, she spoke of them, she could have had lovers.

Is it always like this? For everybody?

Nobody ever speaks of it. But it must be.

On Level Four, they paused at a desk with a chronometer behind it, and pressed their ident disks against it, watching the patterns—individual as thumbprints—flare on the telltales. A pleasant voice came from the desk:

"Ramie, you're wanted on the Bridge level, please. Gildoran, please report to the Nursery level."

"Duty tonight? We must be closer to Liftoff than I thought," Gildoran commented, and Ramie giggled. "They've reprogrammed that thing. It didn't always say *please* like that. Rushka must have had some new psych briefing." She stepped into an elevator; Gildoran took a slidewalk in the opposite direction. Damn, was he set for a spell of Nursery duty? He quailed faintly at the thought. He was fond enough of children, and the little ones growing up kept the ship from being dull in the long stretches between the stars, but he still liked them better once they were housebroken and articulate!

Still, like everyone else, he supposed he had to take his turn at it. He had a faint atavistic wish they'd leave it to the girls—at least biologically they were supposed to have an instinct for it—but he knew that notion was ridiculous, especially on Ship.

The Nursery was in what would be the maximal gravity level of the ship when they were out in space, and had the optimal conditions of light, air, decoration and service. Gildoran paused in front of the translucent glass a moment before entering, watching a small group of three children—a nine-year-old and two five-year-olds—sitting on the floor having their supper, raptly listening to a story told by one of the huge, fuzzy brown humanoids who went, for some reason nobody on the Ships knew, by the name of Poohbears. One of the big creatures saw Gildoran through the wall, signalled for the children to go on with their meal, and waddled toward the doorway, puffing in spite of the extra oxygen rations in the Nursery level. Sinuous and free-moving in the low-gravity ship conditions of space, they were clumsy on a planet, dragging themselves along slowly.

The Poohbear said in her sweet silvery voice "Gildoran, Rae wants you back at the Nursery office, could you go back there directly and not disturb the children?"

"I will. Thanks, Pooh," he said with an affectionate smile. He supposed it was some sort of hereditary memory or something, but the Poohbears were everyone's perfect mother image. Maybe, he thought, it's just imprinting; after all, they're the first mothers any Explorer ever knows. They were the one race not bleached by space, and their long dark fleece remained untouched and obstinately dark brown. On every Explorer ship, they were the specialist-experts with the babies.

In the Nursery office, Gilrae—the Biological Officer for this year—was looking through a group of records, and frowning over them. She had already discarded the planet-wear and was wearing the shipboard Explorer costume of a narrow support-band around her breasts and a narrow kilt about her hips, with thin sandals strapped low on her ankles. It was hard to tell her age; she had not changed since Gildoran could remember, she had been his first teacher when he was eight years old, but she looked little older than Ramie. Now her face was drawn and Gildoran fancied, with surprise, that she had been weeping.

Did she find something—or someone—here that she can't bear to leave?

She raised her head and said "Doran, you're back early. I thought you'd be at the Ceremonial Leavetaking."

"I intended to, but at the last moment I didn't."

She tapped the Record scanner before her. She said "We're going to be shorthanded, Doran. I just had word. Gilmarin went by Transmitter to Head Centre—they sent us word of new Galactic maps—and he must have made a routing mistake; he hasn't been heard of. And Giltallen is . . ." she stopped and swallowed, hard. "He left a message. He's not coming back."

Gildoran felt an answering catch of breath.

"Tallen. How could he? He's been with us—how old is he? He's *old*——"

"It happens." Now Gildoran understood Rae's tears. In a sudden, intense surge of loyalty, he went and put his arms around the older woman. "Rae, don't cry. Maybe he'll change his mind, there are a couple of hours still——"

"He won't. He's been talking about it for years now . . . and once a planet gets hold of you . . ." Rae sobbed, once then struggled to control herself. She said steadily, "We can't judge him."

But I can. I do. I was tempted, too. But here I am . . .

Rae said, "I thought we were going to lose you too, Gildoran."

Silently he shook his head. Now that he was aboard again, now that he was among the familiar things of his life, Janni seemed a brief madness.

Different, not part of my world. . . .

"Planets are for saying goodbye," he said.

Her smile was faint and weak. "You're sure? Because I have to send you out again, everyone else is needed for last liftoff check. Have you ever been to the Hatchery on Antares Four?"

"Are we short?"

Rae nodded, looked around to where a little girl of twelve was working at the files and said, "Gillori, I'm parched, run out and fetch me something to drink, precious." The child ran out of the Section, and Rae said, "We're desperately short, Doran. Remember, only two of the last batch survived, and only one before that. Lori is twelve, which means she can take an apprentice position in a year, but we've had bad luck. Our crew strength is down to forty, and only four children under fifteen. And . . . you know as well as I do that some of the Elders won't be able to handle full duty shifts for a full fifteen years more. We ought to have four or five youngsters, ready to take over."

Doran nodded. From his childhood he had been trained to think in terms of five-year, eight-year, ten-year voyages.

"You'll have to make the Hatchery trip."

Gildoran started with surprise. Normally only the older members of the ship's crew were sent on lengthy Transmitter errands. But Gilrae was speaking as if this were a simple one-planet hop to fetch fruits for supper.

"The *Gypsy Moth* has special Extended Credit through Head Centre," she told him, "and the Antares Hatchery works with us. We ought to have at least six babies; try to get them at six weeks old and with a full month of biological mothering; and birthed, not hatched."

Gildoran gulped. He said, "How in the sixteen Galaxies do I *carry* six yowling kids through four Transmitter laps?"

Gilrae laughed. "Rent a Baby-Haul, of course. And take Ramie with you." Her face was suddenly very serious. "Doran. Get a Cleared Explorer Route from Head Centre. We think Gilmarin tried to plot his own route and strayed on to one of the worlds where they still

17

... don't like Explorers. Never forget; one rock thrown, six hours delay—and you're gone. You could be a hundred years gone."

Her words sobered Gildoran like a faceful of ice-water. All his life he had known this ... *miss a liftoff and you're gone forever.* But Gilmarin had been his playmate —picked up on the same world as Gildoran, surviving the intensive operations which allowed the Explorers to survive in space with him, his Nurserymate until they were ten, his companion ever since—and now he was gone; irrevocably gone, lost somewhere in the thousands of inhabited worlds in space. ...

"Rae, can't we put a tracer on him, send someone out after him? Head Centre could trace his Transmitter co-ordinates ..."

Rae's pale narrow face went taut. Like all Explorers she was colorless, but her eyes were large and violet, and they seemed now to fill her face. She said almost in a whisper, "We tried, Doran. No luck. We followed the co-ordinates for three planets, and stepped into a riot on Lasselli's World. He must have walked right into the middle of it. All Gilhart and I could do was clear out. Hart applied for Lasselli's World to be blocked to Explorers, but that's like putting up a shield when the meteor shower's over." She reached for his hand. Her fingers were narrow and hard, and seemed to shake slightly. She said "*You* stay off Lasselli's World, Doran. And go straight to the Hatchery and straight back. We can't lose you too."

Gildoran felt faint and sick as he went up to the Bridge level to summon Ramie for help on this mission.

And he had actually thought of deserting his people, when they were so short-handed?

When Gilmarin was gone, and Giltallen deserted?

Dismay struggled with anger in him.

They hate us on some worlds, just because we used to take their unwanted, their surplus children. We can't have children of our own. We're sterile from space, we'd breed monsters. Without replacements from the planets we open, we'd have to stop travelling between the stars . . .
And then no more worlds opened, not ever.

And mankind needs a frontier. Without it, even if the known worlds span a Galaxy, mankind psychologically stagnates and goes mad. It was that knowledge that pushed man into space from Old Earth, thousands of years ago. It was that knowledge that lifted him from the swarming, dying, starving, crowded worlds of the First System, pushed him into interstellar space in the days of the old Generation Ships before the Einstein Drives, kept him expanding, going outward. It was what drove mankind to invent the Transmitter; that desperate need for a frontier, to know that they were still able to move onward.

But no one could go to a new world by Transmitter until the Transmitter was first set up there. There was no way to Transmit a Transmitter. Once the *first* Transmitter was established on a planet, anything could be brought through; people, supplies, building materials, anything from any other world which already had a Transmitter on it.

But new worlds still had to be found.

And the Explorers found them. Only the Explorers still travelled between the stars, at the Einstein-Drive speeds which telescoped time for them, and set up new Transmitters for the endless outward expansion of the human race.

And because we used to have to steal children, they hate us.
We have to steal them, beg them, or buy them.
And when they go with us they're gone forever.
FOREVER.

He stepped off the elevator at the Bridge level. On the Bridge, half a dozen crew members were working around the computers; Gildoran gave his message and the Year-Captain, Gilharrad (who was so old that even Gildoran could not imagine how many years it would be in planetary time) dismissed Ramie to accompany him. His eyes, almost lost in crinkles, reached into unguessable gulfs of memory.

"I was nearly killed once on a child-stealing expedition when I was your age," he said, holding out a withered hand that trembled faintly, "Look, I lost this finger from a knife-thrust, and that was so long ago, planet-time, that they didn't even have regeneration to re-grow one for me. We took nineteen babies on that raid, hit three worlds. Of course, that was back when eight out of ten died in the first liftoff and one out of thirty lived more than a month, we didn't even name them until we were sure they'd make it. People haven't changed much, though. They'd still like to kill us, most worlds, if we ask for their children. Even the extra children, the ones they don't want. We're only a legend, on most worlds. But a legend they hate." He fell silent, his old eyes sliding away into the remoteness again. Gildoran, feeling an obscure urge to comfort the ancient, said, "We're dealing with licensed Hatcheries this time. We can simply buy what we need, from people who have a right to sell."

Harrad said, with dim bitterness, "Slavery too. Wait and see. On that one world they may be going through a period of enlightenment—or cynicism. Go back there next time we land—sixty, eighty years planet-time—and I'll bet you a planet-sized fee that they've got it written in their license, *no selling to Explorers.*" He made a feeble movement toward the door. "Better get going, you two. You probably have to take the long way round, and we lift at midnight."

II

Gildoran and Gilramie emerged at the top of the steps, now wrapped in the all-purpose Travel Cloaks. Standards of decency in clothing varied from world to world, so that every psychological type could find a world where they felt comfortable. On some planets nakedness was the norm and clothing considered vaguely insulting, as if you wanted to hide yourself; on others, it was believed that too much bodily exposure blunted sexual drives, destroyed pleasure, so that concealment while you went about your day's work sharpened the impact of exposure in intimate conditions. But the Travel Cloaks were accepted everywhere as the sign that you were in transit and not deliberately flouting local custom.

As they made their way toward the tall dark pylons of the Transmitter Station, Gildoran glanced at the raw-beamed city. Was Janni still there? It did not matter to him now; their parting had been too final for him to cherish any hopes of a reunion. Anyhow, by now she could be fourteen planets away, or at the other end of the Galaxy. With infinite transit available to all, only desire could keep lovers together, and for Janni this had failed; Gildoran relentlessly turned his back on the city and his attention back to Ramie, small and smiling at his side.

"Did Rae say whether we should get males or females, Doran?"

"What difference does it make?" Gildoran smiled down at her. "It's chance anyhow." Aboard the Explorer ships, both sexes took their turns at all tasks, from Navigation to Nursery, and besides, you could never tell how many would survive. Gildoran and Gilmarin had been part of a lot of seven, four girls and three boys: two boys survived. They would probably take three boys and three girls. If they were fortunate, two of each would survive the first month in space; statistically survival rates were now at two out of three. But statistics didn't always work. Twelve years from now, the survivors would be apprentices in every field aboard the Ships. Whatever they were, boy or girl, they would be Explorers.

The two Explorers, tall and pale, shrouded in their Travel Cloaks, passed under the archways of the Transmitter Station. This late in the evening, the crowds had lessened somewhat; at the edge of each booth the lines were shorter than usual. A few merry couples with the look of dissipation, on their way to—or from—an evening of pleasure somewhere. A solitary Drifter or two, emerging for a look at the planet, with the usual look of bewilderment—Drifters took the dangerous route of punching co-ordinates at random for the thrill of reaching unknown worlds. A group of youngsters, looking sleepy, arriving for a guided tour under the chaperonage of two tall green-skinned governesses; probably a group of young adventurers bound for a survival-skills course on this new world.

Gildoran stopped at an information booth and laid his ident disk against the routing plate, punching a request for Routing Services. After the expected three-quarter-second lag, a disembodied voice demanded in Universal "Nature of routing request, please."

23

"A cleared route for Explorers to Antares Four, please."

Again the lag, then the computer began to chatter out the required information, sets of Transmitter co-ordinates. Gildoran put a small coin in the slot—information was free, but a printout of the information cost a small fee—he didn't care to take the chance of forgetting a vital factor in the co-ordinates and arriving on a planet six hundred light-years from his destination!

They stepped inside the glassed-in and green-lighted Transmitter booth, seeing without much attention the rules printed in the two official languages of the Galactic civilization;

STAND FIRMLY ON PLATE

REMEMBER TO RECLAIM YOUR IDENT DISK WHEN LEAVING

BABIES UNDER ONE YEAR OF AGE AND UN- TRAINED ANIMALS MUST BE TRANSMIT- TED INSIDE APPROVED SKINNER BOXES

ELDERLY OR FEEBLE PERSONS SHOULD HAVE A LIFE-SUPPORT HANDY FOR BOOST- ING UNFAMILIAR OXYGEN LEVELS

NO MORE THAN THREE ADULT BEINGS MAY BE TRANSMITTED IN ANY ONE BOOTH

THIS BOOTH FOR PASSENGER TRAVEL ONLY. FOR TRANSPORT OF FREIGHT, CARGO, OR HOUSEHOLD POSSESSIONS WEIGHING OVER APPROVED ALLOTMENT OF EIGHTY UNIVERSAL KILOS, USE BOOTHS AT FAR END OF STATION

ATOMIC DEVICES MAY BE TRANSPORTED ONLY WITH SPECIAL PERMIT FROM PLAN- ET OF DESTINATION

He touched the buttons carefully for the first set of

Co-ordinates. A warning light glowed and the booth went dark for an instant.

Every time he used the Transmitter, Gildoran was briefly conscious of extended space. He had wondered, now and then, if it had anything to do with the mental disciplines of the Explorers or his familiarity with the sensation of time-dilation inside the Ships; or if it were hallucination, imagination, or a freak stimulation of brain cells from the Transmitter. After all, the Transmitters fed on energy drawn from the very fabric of space itself, the drifting matter free between Solar systems. He did not know what caused it; he did not know if other Explorers felt it, or if indeed it was common to everyone who used the Transmitter. He only knew that always, in that moment when the booth went dark, that instant of lag which prevented exact simultaneity. . . .

The booth went dark. A sharp dizziness stung the roots of his nose, a tracery of colors flared in his brain, a retinal swirl of brilliance behind his eyes not too unlike the side-effect of drugs which kept them all sane during time-dilation; and again the strange sense of standing among swirling atoms—or galaxies. . . .

A sharp *snap* like a brief, not unpleasant electric shock; then he came to rest *(had he moved at all?)* knowing that three-quarters of a second had passed and he stood in another Transmitter booth with the identical admonitions facing him, this time in electric-blue neon lights, and now the walls were glassy-green rather than glassy-blue, and he was four light-years away from the planet he had just left. He shook his head slightly, glanced at Gilramie—did she look a little dizzy too?— and consulted the printout for the next set of co-ordinates on their route. The Transmitter, strictly speaking,

25

had no limit; but it was more pleasant for most people not to jump more than four light-years in one Transmission, and the power-consumption, for some unknown reason, went up exponentially beyond that level; so that jumps much longer than that were not recommended except for the highest-priority personnel. Too long a jump seemed, for some psychological reason no one had ever figured out, to have an effect not unlike that of too-fast jet travel. So long trips were routed into short steps of four light-years at a time, where possible. Possibly, Gildoran thought, the human mind can't really absorb the idea of jumping much more than four light-years at a time.

Four more jumps, with brief swirls of darkness between them, and they reached the planet of Antares Four where the Hatchery was located. A map of the planet, and a jump by short-range Transmitter, brought them within a few streets of it.

It was a large glass-and-metal building, with streaming advertisers floating on the air around it, and solidographs of what seemed like hundreds of chubby smiling babies of every size, color and human phenotype. Ramie smiled at the insubstantial infants and said, "I wonder if they're all as cute as this? Don't they have any homely or cranky or bawling ones?"

Gildoran chuckled. "Certainly not on the advertising posters."

A featureless servomech beckoned them in and said in a gentle, cultured voice, "Welcome, gentlebeings and prospective parents. Will you please wait in this area, and one of our salesbeings will be with you in a brief time. Meanwhile, we invite you to look at the literature describing our newest service." The servo's flexible metal arms thrust some leaflets at them and it glided away. Gildoran glanced at it;

NOW, your favorite HATCHERY offers a NEW SERVICE! Are you tired of waiting six months for a baby to your order? Women, you now can escape nine months of missed pleasures, troublesome births, suicidal and dangerous postpartum depressions! You've decided you'd rather not adopt, so what to do? NOW, you can stop by for a simple painless visit, leave your one-to-four-week fertilized fetus with us, and for a modest fee you can be guaranteed absolutely against fetal insult, birth defects or deformities; if for any reason your baby isn't absolutely perfect we hatch you another one FREE!

Smaller lettering read;

DNA surgery, guaranteed talents, or sex preference at a small additional fee. Ask us about bargains in unclaimed or rejected hatches.

Ramie was looking through an identical leaflet. "This isn't any good to us. We need them birthed, not hatched, and with a full month of biological mothering."

Gildoran nodded. "Rae gave me the specifications. Ramie, ask about musical talent. If Tallen really has gone. . . ." He didn't finish; he didn't have to. Giltallen had been the best musician—Rae herself excepted—aboard *Gypsy Moth*. He looked around the waiting room, also filled with advertising solidos, drifting through the air, of chubby smiling infants.

A thick-set fussy small man bustled in. "Well, well, prospective parents, what can we do for you today—oh, Explorers. I suppose you'll be wanting a quantity?"

Gildoran put his question about musical talent, and the small man's face lighted up.

"Why, as it happens, I have just the one you want. The mother was a top-grade harpist, who paid for study on Capella Nine with Ligettini himself by having five children for me—one every year. She'd study all year, come

27

here and birth them, give them the full month of biological mothering—these are absolutely top-grade merchandise—get impregnated again with sperm from top-level
musical geniuses each with a prepotency factor of nine,
and go off to study again during her pregnancy. All of
them but this one were pre-sold, some of them ordered
four years in advance. But the last couple had their
hearts set on a girl, and she birthed a boy, and they're
from one of those religious-fanatic planets which prohibit
sex-change operations. Heartbreaking, really, but I can
make you this absolutely splendid offer . . ." he men-
tioned a sum in stellars which struck Gildoran as not too
exorbitant. He glanced at Ramie.

"Let's take that one," she said, "it would please Rae so
much."

The little man riffled through a folder, and his face
fell. "Sorry, gentlebeings," he said ruefully, "there's a
hold on that one. To be sold only to a "stable couple"—
no entertainment-mongers, pleasure worlds or—I'm
sorry—Explorer Ships. But look here, you people from
the Ships want quantity. I can give you a wonderful boy
on ten cloned High-IQ Hatches. Quality absolutely
guaranteed, we aren't one of those places which sell off
our dud merchandise to you people just because we
know you can't come back and complain about them!"

Gildoran felt faintly sickened. *Merchandise!* And did
they want cloned identicals, even High-IQ? He didn't
think so. The interpersonal relationships aboard ship
were loosely polarized, often shifting; identicals—ten of
them, horrors!—might form a clique of their own, or
worse, be so much alike in personality that they would
be too uninteresting. Imagine having ten of the same
person, making up one-fifth of the crew? Suppose they
grew up with some unlikeable personality trait?

"No thanks," he said, groped for an excuse, and hit quickly upon a true one. "We need them birthed, not hatched. And individuals, not clones."

"Oh, come now," said the little man, deprecatingly, "don't tell me you people, with your scientific disciplines, have that old superstition that birthed babies are better than hatched ones?"

"For our purpose they *are* better," Gilramie said in her soft voice, "Somehow the experience of full pregnancy closeness, and the month of biological mothering, gives them a better ability for imprinting and forming interpersonal relations. And this also adds to their will to live; hatched babies tend to die quickly in space because they don't immediately form an attachment with a mother figure and have less desire to survive."

"Well, you know your own business best, I suppose," the little man said. "Why don't you stroll through the warehouse and look around, while I wait on someone else? This one will be quick, I've waited on her before, and maybe you'll see something that takes your fancy." He opened the door to an enormous room, stretching into the distance, filled with boxes of one-way-glass; the modern version of the "Skinner Box" which kept an infant dry, fed, and entertained without human intervention for up to twenty hours at a time. The room was filled with the soft thumping heartbeat-sound which was known to keep infants content. Behind the glass walls babies gurgled, kicked, crawled, howled or suckled. They seemed happy, although Gildoran wondered if they could really be happy as the babies aboard *Gypsy Moth* were happy, continually mothered and tended by the Poohbears.

"Specifications on the front of each box," the salesman said. "I'll be with you in a minute or two, this will be quick."

He went off to an enormously tall, sallow, but somehow enticing woman, wrapped in a travel cloak but with lovely streaming hair and a walk Gildoran could not take his eyes off.

"Yes, Gentlebeing?"

The woman's voice, very sweet and exquisitely trained, reached them from a distance;

"I need six prime females with empath potential and musical talent, high sexuality potential. These are to be trained as top-level pleasure-girls, so make certain they are pretty ones."

The salesman scurried around, making up an order form, while Gildoran struggled against his initial revulsion. *Slavery!* And yet . . . these "prime females" would be pampered all their lives, beautiful and happy. . . .

The salesman was trying to push up the sale;

"Throw in a fine bargain on some distress merchandise —unclaimed hatches, wonderful condition but they're already six months old, so they're past imprinting. But they'll make fine manual workers or servants, all healthy and guaranteed good-natured, no genetic defects! Take 'em off my hands at a flat two thousand stellars for the three!"

When the salesperson came back, Gildoran and Ramie had chosen six from the specifications on the boxes; all were guaranteed high-IQ, with mathematical and mechanical ability, two were from families of surgeons on either side, and two were of hereditary lines with musical talent. Phenotype or skin color, of course, didn't matter; after two years they'd be Explorers anyway. Hard radiation as faster-than-light speeds would take care of that.

He watched the servos piling the infants bound for the pleasure-world into a tall wheeled structure which looked like a stack of small Skinner Boxes piled on top of one another; a standard baby-haul for taking infants through the Transmitter. He asked abruptly, "How can you have the heart to sell them into what amounts to a life of prostitution?"

The little man shrugged. He said, "On some worlds, robots are banned, just for that—to make room for people to earn a living by manual labor. What the hell, some places won't sell to *you* because you and I know, about one-third of them will die. Me, I sell them for anything except food—I do draw the line at *that*. A few exclusive places cater to the carriage trade—"

"What's that?"

"Sorry. Old salespeople term—I think a *carriage* was some kind of luxury-class Transmitter in the early days, it means, only sell to luxury trade, all singletons, all for sale to families only. But me, I sell 'em to anyone who can pay for 'em, and I ask no questions, and it's a good thing too—after all, where else would *you* people get babies if we were all that discriminating?"

A legend. But a legend they hate.

The little salesman had gotten himself wound up now.

"After all, there are billions too many babies—most of them we pick up cheap on worlds with a population problem and some freak religion that won't let them solve it, freaky worlds where abortion's illegal or worlds with fertility cults. Better than shipping them off wholesale for slave labor."

"I guess so," Gildoran said apologetically. "Here, I think we want these six." He had noted down the numbers of their display box. "And we'll need to rent a baby-haul; we can ship it back in less than an hour, after they're loaded."

He stood watching the servos load the babies. There

was one, with dark tilted eyes like Ramie's and soft golden skin, that he wished he could pick up and cuddle. Ramie, too, was watching intently. He looked questioningly at her and she murmured, "Oh, nothing. I was just wondering what it would be like to birth my own——"

"Messy, I would think, and it would interfere with ship routine," Gildoran said, deliberately making a joke of it.

Some questions you never asked. Ramie would learn. . . .

While Ramie arranged for rental of the baby haul and servos to tend it for the long and complex route through the Transmitter, back to the world of their departure, Gildoran accompanied the salesperson to a public Computer Station, where he arranged for transfer of credits from Head Centre to the Hatchery. Briefly he contemplated stopping somewhere for a last planetside meal before they returned to the ship. No; they had a longish trip by Transmitter before them—at least three-quarters-of-an-hour, with the necessary hunt for booths large enough to handle a six-baby hauling unit—and the sooner the babies were loaded on to the *Gypsy Moth*, the sooner their troubles would be over.

He had already begun congratulating himself on a successful mission. With the aid of the servos, who were rented ready-programmed, it was easy to find freight-size Transmitter booths. He verified a cleared return route at the Information booth and watched the servos wheel the Baby-haul inside. He and Ramie stood on either side of the tall nest of opaque boxes, which of course had their own air-systems and optimal temperature inside.

He hoped the little golden-skinned girl with the sleek dark hair and slanted dark eyes would live. It would be fun to see her grow up. You didn't dare get attached to them until you were sure they'd live. . . .

The booth darkened; the disorientation and brilliant swirls of retinal circus—atoms? Star-Galaxies?—raced through his brain. *Snap!* They were in the Transmitter booth. His fingers sought out the coordinates of the second jump, but he found himself wondering how the babies experience Transmitter travel? Did they cry or feel shock or fear at the sudden darkening? Was there a sense of telescoped time?

Does a baby experience time at all, I wonder? Or only his own biological rhythms?

He touched the coordinates; again the darkness, the swirling colors, the *snap*. He thought, I'll have to check, find out if others, Ramie, Harrad, Rae, if they sense this in the Transmitter.

It had never occurred to him, to ask Janni.

And yet—we were so close, for a little while. But we had other things to ask each other.

The third jump; the third darkness-swirl-*snap* gestalt. And it struck him then, with a sense of irrevocable loss, that now he would never be able to ask Gilmarin—his playmate, the lost, the vanished—about this. NEVER. That word again. Gilmarin, his nurserymate-brother-playmate, that he would never be able to find out whether Gilmarin shared this individual disorientation in the Transmitter, suddenly it struck him as greater tragedy than the now-very-small loss of Janni.

Janni and I shared—a planet. Gilmarin and I shared a life, and I've lost them both. When Janni left me I felt as if I'd lost something wonderful, and I had; my dreams about her.

But with Gilmarin I lost a piece of myself, wandering forever, as he is lost and wandering somewhere in a thousand thousand other worlds where I can never go. . . .

"Doran . . ." Ramie's light voice wavered and sounded frightened, "Are you sure the co-ordinates were right? Something seems to be wrong."

Snapping sharply to full attention, Gildoran checked the coordinates of the booth; an override light was blinking and the coordinates on the tell-tale did not match those on the printout in his hand. He touched the proper set of coordinates again, spelling them out firmly with his fingers and verifying them again on the visual tell-tale before pressing the ACTIVATE button. . . . one of the many fail-safe devices which the Transmitter provided to keep careless travellers from pressing non-existent co-ordinates to materialize in an unknown destination. The booth did not activate, and a light began to blink and spell out words above them;

FOR REASONS OF EXTRA-HEAVY TRAFFIC PATTERNS ALL TRAVELLERS IN THIS SECTOR ARE BEING RE-ROUTED TO DESTINATIONS ELSEWHERE ON THEIR ULTIMATE ROUTE. PLEASE CHECK WITH THE PUBLIC INFORMATION BOOTH AT THE FAR END OF THE STATION FOR A FREE RE-ROUTING PRINTOUT. WE APOLOGIZE FOR THE INCONVENIENCE AND REASSURE ALL TRAVELLERS THAT THOSE ARRIVING UN-REQUESTED ON THIS WORLD NEED NOT CHECK FOR

CONTRABAND; REPEAT, ALL CONTRABAND REGULATIONS HAVE BEEN TEMPORARILY SUSPENDED FOR THE DURATION OF THE TRAVEL EMERGENCY PROVIDED YOU DEPART WITHIN ONE PLANETARY HOUR OF ARRIVAL.

Gildoran muttered an archaic vulgarism. "That's all we need."

Ramie asked, "What's contraband?"

"This must be one of the freaky planets—the ones that prohibit importation of servos or slaves or drugs or fissionables. Contraband means a substance prohibited by law on this special planet. But relax; it doesn't apply to us anyhow because we're in transit and we arrived here without intending to. We'll have to go and get the rerouting printout."

They stepped out of the booth, Gildoran bending down to peer through the window of the baby-haul. The translucent windows showed only that two were asleep, the others moving around; the soundproof box made it impossible to tell whether they were crying or not, but Gildoran knew that if they were hungry they would be fed, and that they would be kept amused if awake, so there was no need to worry about them for awhile at least. He looked around, orienting himself in the Transmitter station; they were all laid out to a standard pattern (this was so that the traveller could find, with a minimum of trouble, food or clothing or bathrooms, information or service.)

"What planet are we on?" Gilramie asked.

Gildoran shrugged. "How in time should I know? Somewhere between Antares Four and the planet where we left *Gypsy Moth*, obviously, which cuts it down to a couple of hundred. Stay here by the booth, Ramie.

There's no point in moving the baby-haul through the whole station."

She looked uneasily at the crowd. She said "Gildoran, I don't like it here much. Maybe it's just that stuff about contraband, but it evidently isn't a very free place. Can't we jump straight to the *Gypsy Moth?* I know those coordinates by heart, and so do you. Would it really hurt the babies to do it?"

"I don't know. Probably not, but I just don't know," Gildoran said. "The risk is supposed to be psychological, and as far as I know, nobody ever studied the effects of long jumps on babies. Just the same, it's likely to be an awfully unpleasant experience. I made a twenty-light-year jump once, and it wasn't any fun. I was dizzy for an hour afterward, and I could hardly see. Why give the poor brats traumas before we've had them half an hour? It won't take three minutes to get the re-routing."

"Well, all right . . ." she said uncertainly. He walked away toward the far end of the station, through a half-seen crowd of people.

They edged back. They always did. He would only have noticed if they hadn't . . . you never looked at the crowds and the stares, you learned early never to take any notice . . .

"Dirty baby-stealer!" somebody yelled, "Hey, look, another one! They got their nerve!"

"LET'S GET THEM!"

Gildoran, jerked out of his habitual arrogant lack-of-notice, looked round him like a trapped animal. Someone jostled him; someone kicked; he was surrounded by a crowd pushing in, fighting. . . .

He bellowed, in the ship-language of the Explorers no

one else could understand, "Ramie! Take the kids and *jump!* Get back to the *Gypsy Moth*—all the way—FAST!" He turned, by instinct leading them away from her . . . they hadn't seen her yet. His arm shot out; he kicked a man on the kneecap and the man howled and fell at his feet. He butted through the crowd; cast one swift look back: Ramie and the baby-haul were gone.

Something snapped into awareness in his brain. *Lasselli's World!* Just a set of co-ordinates on a Transmitter route-map, but he knew enough to stay away from it—that was what had been wrong. Gilmarin would never have gone there knowingly, but the random bad luck of a computer re-routing traffic patterns had sent him there, just as it had sent himself and Ramie. . . .

Well, the babies and Ramie were safely away, vanished into the booth; light-years away by now. He kicked, elbowed, butted through the crowd, fighting his way through a volley of blows and curses, struggling to stay on his feet. If he went down he was done for, he'd be trampled. . . .

"Kill the dirty Explorer! He won't steal any more babies here and kill on his ships!"

"Get back!" There was the crackle of a heat-gun. Gildoran felt the crowd subside, draw away; leaving him standing in a cleared space before a dark-skinned youth in some kind of uniform with epaulets, and a baldric with an unknown emblem. He held the drawn heat-gun in his hand and the menace was obvious. The mob, thwarted, muttered and pushed; but it let the dark youngster through to Gildoran.

The stranger said in Universal, "Come with me, Explorer. We'll handle this legally." His voice crackled at the crowd like the snap and zip of his weapon; "Get away from him! I'll handle this!"

Gildoran drew himself up and managed to summon

some remnants of his habitual arrogance, although he realized that his clothing was ripped and torn, his face bleeding from a blow. He said to the dark young man, "I protest. You have no authority over me. I was re-routed here by computer override and all contraband regulations are legally suspended. I demand an immediate appeal to Head Centre."

"You aren't going to demand anything," the stranger said tonelessly. "Come with me."

"You have no authority——"

"*This* is my authority," said the youth, making a minute gesture with the heat-gun. "I'd rather not use it here. Come with me." He said in an undertone, between clenched teeth, "Damn it, man, come *on*, I can't hold them long, do you want to be *lynched?* They killed one of you here today!"

Gildoran went, hearing the mutter of the crowd rising and knowing what the young stranger said was true. *Gilmarin! Had he died here?* Gildoran felt a sob strangling in his throat and set his mouth hard. *Die like an Explorer.* Marin would have done just that. He could, too, if he had to. He held his head high as they walked outside the station.

They stepped into the blinding light of a double blue-white sun; Gildoran squeezed his eyes shut, looking through squinched lids at his captor. The strange uniformed man was more than a full head shorter than he, narrowly bearded, but looking no older than Gildoran himself; skin and hair were shiny black, but his eyes were a warm, lustrous animal brown. He let the heat-ray drop slightly and said "I thought I'd never get you out of there. Why did you try to fight me? You're safer in custody than with a mob. I'm not going to hurt you." His thick lips parted in a grin. "I've got no authority to. My job is shooting escaped snakes from the forest preserve—

38

that's where I got the uniform and the weapon—fortunately that mob hasn't realized it yet. Lucky I was in the station. Did you come here to rescue that poor devil they got today?"

Gildoran shook his head, and his face must have shown something, for the man said compassionately, "Friend of yours?"

"Shipmate. Best friend," Gildoran said briefly.

Anyway Ramie had gotten away with the babies; even if he was lost, the ship wouldn't be dangerously short-handed.

He said, summoning all his authority, speaking as he did from the Navigation post on the bridge of the *Gypsy Moth*, "I'm grateful to you for getting me away from that lynch mob. But now I really must insist that you get me through to Head Centre without delay. I must rejoin my ship at once."

Even if they don't kill me . . . delay me four hours and I'm dead to the only world that matters. . . .

The young man looked concerned. He slipped his weapon into its holster and said, "That's right, you Explorers can never dare miss a ship, can you? I've read everything I can find about you. I . . . I'm interested. Look, we mustn't stay here, if anyone in the mob steps out and finds us chatting like old cronies I'll just be lynched alongside you, and my heat-gun won't really do all that much good—there isn't even a lethal setting for humans on it. Come on—hurry!"

He drew him along quickly, through a winding side street, and Gildoran went for a moment without protesting, but then dug in his heels.

"No! I can't risk losing myself here, losing sight of the Transmitter on a strange world——"

"You've got to trust me," the youngster implored, and drew him into the lee of a wall.

"Look here, you evidently don't understand the political situation here on Lasselli's World, and I haven't the time to explain. Let it go at this; if you went in to the formal authorities and asked to be put through to Head Centre, you'd never make it. And they'll be expecting you to try and sneak back to that Transmitter station— I'd bet you a hundred stellars, if I had them, that there's someone from that mob watching every door, ready to raise a riot. There's a gang here trying to control Transmitter travel—yes, I know that Head Centre has ruled that illegal, but we're a long way from Head Centre. The facts of the matter are that with the Transmitter, anyone who doesn't like a given political regime can step into a Transmitter and be at the other end of the Galaxy in a few minutes, so local citizens are subject to spot-checks and searches at the main Transmitter stations, and off-worlders tend to be hustled and rousted so they won't talk to our people and make them discontented. And unhappy people need something to hate—right now, you're it."

Gildoran said, "So what do I do?"

The man said, "I have an idea. It won't be easy, but we may be able to manage it. My name's Merrik, by the way; what's yours?"

"Gildoran of the *Gypsy Moth*."

"Well, Gildoran, they'll be expecting you to react just as you did—afraid to get far away from the Transmitter station, afraid to risk getting lost, so they'll be waiting, thinking you'll risk anything to try to slip back in, maybe in disguise. The one thing they *won't* expect is that you'll be able to get to another Transmitter station, maybe fifty kilos away. Oh, they may keep a half an eye on public transit, but they won't expect you to have help. So maybe we can fool them. How much time do you actually have? It isn't a matter of minutes, is it?"

Gildoran checked the chronometer on his wrist, which registered time on the *Gypsy Moth's* planet whatever local time might be. He felt queer to realize that it was, to him, early evening while here it was obviously only half way through the morning. "No, I have about three planetary hours, objective time."

Merrik let out a breath of relief. "Oh, well. That's easily managed. Here, come through this back alley, I'll get you to my apartments, we've got to do something about your skin and hair before you try going out on any public street."

Gildoran, stunned and relieved, followed him. Inside a small lift to Merrik's rooms in a rabbit-warren of a building, he said, "Why are you doing this?"

Merrik shrugged, a little sheepishly. He said, "I'm interested in the Explorers. Fascinated by them. Sometimes I think you're the only real adventurers left. The idea of standing wholly free of time as you do. . . ."

Gildoran blinked; that was a strange viewpoint on it, whereas he thought of earthworms, planet-dwellers, as living outside the drag of time as he did, going from star to star in the blink of an eye—literally—while the Explorers crawled between stars by the Einstein-drive. He tried to say something of this; Merrik, opening the lift door with a cautious look down the hall and hurrying Gildoran inside, said "But think of it this way. We live our whole biological lifespan inside absolute, objective time. I was born nineteen years ago, and eighty-some years from now I'll die, having lived the fivescore years man's expected to live, and I have no idea, except from my reading and study, what the Universe was like a hundred years before I was born, and I'll never—never —*never* know what the Universe will be five hundred years from now. But you were born maybe five hundred years ago; you lived in a time that's only history to me, and your lifespan can go thousands of years into the future, in that same fivescore allotted years of man!"

Gildoran had never thought of it like this. Merrik was rummaging behind panels, pulling out some garments. "You're too tall to wear breeches, but I have a travel cloak that I bought on Rigel III, just swap it for yours. Here, this will handle the skin and hair." He sat Gildoran on a low seat and began rubbing him efficiently with a greenish paste which, surprisingly, dried purplish-black on his skin. He sprayed his hair with some stuff from an aerosol globe.

"Now you just look like a slightly oversized Lasselli. Here, rub it into your hands, up to the elbows, and your feet up to the knees, the cloak will cover up the rest. What race are your people originally, what world did the Explorers come from?"

Gildoran looked at him in surprise. He thought everyone knew. "All worlds," he said. "We have men from everywhere, and women too."

"You're joking, surely? You all have the same coloring, the same physique——"

"Radiation in space does that, and low-grav conditions on the ships. I might have been as black as you when I was a baby."

Merrik grinned uneasily. He said, "Trying to tell me we're brothers under the skin? Well, we look it now, all right, except that your eyes are blue. So it's radiation, eh? But doesn't it affect your children? Or is it a true mutation that breeds true?"

Gildoran said in astonishment, "But we can't have children, the Explorers are all sterile. Man, why do you think we buy them, and used to steal them sometimes?"

Merrik was open-mouthed. He said, "But no one seems to know that, most people think it's for some religious rite——"

"No," Gildoran said impatiently, "they simply become . . . our children. The only children we have. We were bringing six from a hatchery, my friend and I. One of them might be our captain thirty years from now."

Merrik looked at him in deep sympathy. He said "Why don't you tell people?"

"We've told them," Gildoran said wearily, "told them and told them. But we can't tell a thousand thousand worlds with a million people on each, and evidently legends are more durable than facts."

"We have a saying," Merrik said, "Truth crawls at light-speed; lies travel by Transmitter." He smiled and stood up, "Let me pour you a drink, my friend. And then, speaking of speed, we'd better make some. I have a surface-sled, a small airfoil; it belongs to my sister, but she's off-planet on her honeymoon and left it for me to use. I can get you to the Transmitter station fifty miles away. They'll never look for you there—and if they do look for you, they'll never know you. I doubt if your own mother would—no, you don't have mothers, then? Your own shipmates won't know you. In fact, with you disguised like this, you could probably walk right back into the Transmitter station we left, but they just *might* be on the alert there for an extra-tall man."

Gildoran drank down the tingling liquid Merrik poured; it left him feeling vaguely euphoric and refreshed. They went down by lift to the garage where Merrik's surface vehicle was parked. The garage held a stray dozen men and women, but none of them gave Gildoran more than an offhand glance; he clutched his cloak tightly round him lest it blow aside and reveal undyed skin. Merrik helped him strap into the seat of the airfoil car and they were off, skimming low above the surface of the planet.

Surface travel was something almost new to Gildoran. He sat back, feeling the wind blow through his hair and against his face, slitting his eyes against the blinding brilliance of the double sun. The sky was brilliant white, with clouds almost electric-blue.

Such a beautiful world to hold such ugliness. And such kindness.

Merrik said, and to Gildoran his voice sounded a little wistful, "This is the closest I'll ever come to space travel. When humanity got the Transmitter, we gained the ability to *travel* between stars, but we lost the stars themselves. Sometimes I dream about them—about the stars."

"You have the freedom of a thousand thousand planets, Merrik. Each time I leave one I can never go back."

"But they're all . . . *planets*," Merrik half whispered, and his eyes were full of longing. "Space is gone. No one but you Explorers have it now."

They brought the airfoil to rest in front of another Transmitter station. This one was almost unoccupied; they walked in with no one taking the slightest notice of Gildoran with his darkened skin and long cloak. Gildoran went toward a booth. He said "I'll jump straight through to the *Gypsy Moth*. Merrik—how can I ever thank you?" He took the young man's hands in his own.

On this world he had lost a friend. On this world he had found a friend, and now would lose him, too. . . .

Merrik said "Let me go with you. I'd like to see one of your ships. Up close."

Gildoran put a hand on his shoulder. "Come along then."

Inside the booth he punched the familiar co-ordinates and braced himself for the long jump.

Darkness. A swirl of dizzying lights, like the drift of stars in space . . . strange pain at the root of his nose and in his ears . . . spinning galaxies, disoriented, whirling . . .

Snap!

With relief, he saw that they were back on the familiar world of the *Gypsy Moth*. Merrik was standing beside him, still looking dazed. He said "That's the longest jump I ever made, in one leap."

Gildoran's head hurt. He said "I'm sorry, really. But I don't have a lot of time to spare, and my . . . my shipmates will be worrying about me."

Rae. She must be in a real panic, Marin gone, Tallen deserted. Gods grant Ramie's back safely with the children.

He drew Merrik along, saying "I've time to let you have a look at the Ship, though. It's the least I can do."

The guard at the gate, a middle-aged Explorer with a kind, lined face, stopped them as they came toward it, saying "Sorry. Too near takeoff time. Only Ship's personnel now, boys; no more tourists."

"Gilroth, don't you know me?" Gildoran laughed, held up his ident disk; pulled off the travel cloak.

Roth clutched Gildoran into a smothering bear hug.

"Doran," he gulped, "Doran, you made it, Harrad and Rae are frantic, it was all we could do to keep them from going out after you, and it's getting so late, so late. . . ."

"I ran into a spot of trouble," Gildoran said, carefully casual. "Ramie made it back all right with the kids?"

"Oh, yes; poor child, she hasn't stopped crying since, but the babies are all on board, probably already tucked into the Poohbears pockets for liftoff." The pouches of the huge marsupial humanoids had been found to be safer during takeoff than any artificial-womb or life-support system for infants under three months old. Roth added "Better get aboard, tell Rae and the rest that you're all right. And don't forget to check in at the nursery, either!"

"Just a minute. Merrik helped me escape—I'd never be here without him. I promised him a quick look inside."

"All right, but be quick, and do check with the bridge right away," Roth said, "and have your friend out again in ten minutes, the steps are going to be cleared away."

Gildoran escorted Merrik up the steps. He shook his still-aching head, and Merrik, watching his face, said "You too?" After a minute he said "Sometimes, when I make a long jump, it seems that what I see—behind my eyes—must be like what I would see from space. Could it be that we really *do*, somehow, go through all that space, without being aware of it?"

"I don't know. I'm not sure about the meaning of space and time any more," Gildoran said honestly. He laid his ident disk against the telltale. The pleasant computer voice said "You are late in reporting, Gildoran, please check at once with Rae at the nursery level, I have been asked to inform you that Gilramie has already gone to her post on the bridge. I am also requested to remind the stranger present with you that exactly nine minutes and eighteen seconds remain before ship-sealing."

Gildoran said "I'll give you a quick look at the bridge." He stood quiet while the lift carried them up, slid open; quiet while Merrik looked, with longing eyes, at the be-

46

wildering controls and instruments, the busy figures of the Explorers crew going about their unknown, and to him unknowable, duties. Finally Gildoran touched his shoulder, drew him away and silently conducted him to the steps again.

One more goodbye. Forever.

He laid both his hands on Merrik's shoulders, feeling torn and lost and desperate.

"Gildoran," Merrik said suddenly, "take me with you. As crew. I'll do anything."

Deeply moved, Gildoran shook his head. Above them the sky was dark and the raw new city showed a thousand searing lights; but beyond them were a thousand searing stars. "I wish I could. But you'd die in space, Merrik. You have to be taken on when you're a baby. A year or less. The kind of ships we use now, you have to grow up on them. You wouldn't live a month, and it's a terrible death."

Merrik's dark face worked, but he didn't say anything. He only put a foot on the top step, turning back for an instant to say "Gildoran. When you reach your next world . . . come back again. You know my world. I know it will be a long time, but I won't forget. I swear I won't forget."

Hoarsely, Gildoran said "No, Merrik. No, my friend. You might not forget. But you'd hate me. You'd be an old man, and I'd still be young, still the age we are now. Goodbye, Merrik." He blinked back tears as Merrik wrung his hands; then helplessly let him go. He didn't watch him stumble blindly away over the red mud at the foot of the steps. He turned away inside and went dazedly toward the bridge.

It's the effects of the long jump, he thought, clutching his aching head, but he knew it was more.

The tempo of the *Gypsy Moth* was picking up now; alarms rang, crew members—his brothers and friends, his only world—scurried to their stations, the computer's soft voice routed orders here and there. Gildoran turned toward the nursery level, dreading the way Rae would clutch at him and cry over him with anguished gladness at his return, but yet in some way longing for the comfort of it, too. Some day he would tell her the whole story, but not now, not for a long, long time....

The ship was sealed; Gilroth, the last inside, caught up to Gildoran in the corridor. "Well, it's up stakes and out again, lad. Sorry to leave?"

His love. His oldest friend. His newest friend, the only one who had ever understood....

The last of his youth.

"Sorry to leave? Hell no," Gildoran said, "planets are for saying goodbye."

* * *

Something hidden; go and find it
Something lost beyond the ranges....
Lost and waiting for you. Go!
                    Kipling

Part Two

HELLWORLD

I

It lay a thousand miles beneath them, blue and beautiful in their viewscreens, wrapped in a fluffy blanket of pale clouds, drifting endlessly across its face. There were continents and oceans and polar caps.

"Looks like it's got everything a planet ought to have," Raban said, twisting the dials that kept the world below them in focus. "What does it say to you, Doran?"

Gildoran read out the computer data, summarizing as he went. "Plenty of heavy metals. Nickel-iron core. Low radiation background, no Van Allen-type belts worth mentioning. I think this one is going to be it, Raban."

The older man nodded. "We need it," he said. "We're running a little bit low on iron. Pooh Three said some of the babies had a low haemoglobin reading—not low enough to be dangerous, but low enough that we shouldn't pass up a planet with an iron-based chemical structure. Final decision's up to Rae and the Captain, of course, but I think we go in." He got up and stretched. "Let's go break the news."

Gildoran spoke formally to the fifteen-year-old girl at the Communications switchboard; "You have the bridge, Lori." It still felt funny leaving her there alone. He'd spent the last year teaching her the work of her first post, and it had gone so deep in him—you never left a Class C apprentice on the job alone, not even for twenty seconds, not in *any* sector, without a Class A on the job— that he still felt he ought to call someone else to relieve him. He started to ask her if she thought she'd be okay, but fortunately he remembered in time how *he'd* felt on his first post. So he waited for her formal confirmation "I have the bridge," and, without another word, made himself turn away and leave the bridge at Raban's side without a backward glance.

Raban said, as they went down in the lift, "It's about time we found a good one. Many more like the last couple of systems, and we'd be getting into the center of the Nebula. Nothing but frozen giants and dark stars in system after system—and when Rae did find a likely-looking star, its companion picks just *that* time to go Nova. Lucky we were still outside Barricini's Limit, or we'd have been drawn in." He looked grave. "I've always believed that's what happened to the *Golden Hind.* It was eighty years ago, shiptime and we never heard anything except that it hasn't been reported on any known world for two thousand years of their time but when I last talked to a friend from that ship he said they were heading in the direction of the Greater Magellanic Cloud and there were half a dozen stars going Nova in that direction, about then."

Gildoran was too young, shiptime, to remember the *Golden Hind.* It was only a name he'd heard, sometime, somewhere, knowing it was one of the old roster of the Explorer ships.

Once there were a hundred of them. How many are left now, I wonder?

But that was another of the questions you learned never to ask.

Raban said "It's your planet, Gildoran. You want the privilege of telling the Captain about it?"

This was generous of Raban; he could have claimed credit for himself. "Not necessary. We found it together. But before the official word goes out, can I drop down to the Nursery and tell Ramie? I know she's worrying."

Raban smiled, a knowing smile, and said "Sure, you tell her first." And suddenly Gildoran was angry.

"Damn it! I'm sick of this—look, Ramie's working in Nursery. She's worrying about the babies and the haemoglobin levels. I promised, if I got the word, I'd tell her right away. That's all it is. *All.*"

Raban blinked and stared. "Have you two quarreled, Doran?"

He said stiffly "There's no 'us two' to quarrel. No, Ramie and I have always been good friends. I hope we always will be."

That's no lie. We will be again, when Ramie gets over this nonsense . . .

"Look, Gildoran, I'm sorry," Raban said slowly, "I had no intention of getting you mad—or of prying into your business, either. It's only that everybody thinks of you and Ramie in the same breath, almost. Everybody on board *Gypsy Moth* expected that you two would be paired and settled down by now."

"Everyone thought! Everyone expected!" Gildoran burst out. "Maybe that's half the trouble! People have been mentally putting me and Ramie to bed together since we were twelve years old!"

Even Ramie, herself. Dammit, can't she have a little more independence, a little self-respect? Can't she do her own thinking instead of just taking what other people think as gospel?

Raban said slowly "I'm sorry it bothers you, Doran. But look at it from our point of view, can't you? You're almost exactly the same age . . . you're the only two on Ship who *are* the same age, since we lost Gilmarin. If it isn't Ramie you want, who?"

"That's the kind of thinking I mean," Gildoran said desperately, "what difference does age make? It isn't as if we could expect to start a family!" Raban looked shocked and offended as if Gildoran had voiced some blasphemy.

I've broken another taboo!

"Everybody pairing us off just because we happen to have been hatched in the same litter! I thought we were all supposed to be equals aboard Ship, once we're out of the Nursery, the only caste being what office we're holding at the time! Is that true? Isn't that Explorer custom? Or is that just some kind of pretty lie you tell us, and the truth is that you keep all the children together in their play-pens?"

Raban blinked and shook his head. "No," he said. "No, it's not that. You are our equals. You, or Ramie, might be the Captain of *Gypsy Moth* next year and every living soul on this ship would be under your orders. No, Doran. It's only that . . . well . . . I don't know why it's hard to say this, but it is. We're . . . well, we're *sentimental* about you and Ramie, Doran. Maybe it's hard on you. Maybe it makes you feel as if we were intruding into your private affairs. But that's all it is, just sentiment. After all . . ." he looked away, in the narrow shaft, from the younger man, "after all . . . you were our babies."

It was Gildoran's turn to be shocked and to keep silent, while they stepped out of the lift shaft and moved down the corridor.

They were high in the ship now, far out on the rim where gravity was low, kept at minimum for the Elders; the few elder statesmen of the *Gypsy Moth,* too old for work, too old to bear the gravity or stress of a planet. Even when they were on the surface of a world, they were kept within the antigravity fields for their own safety. Gilharrad, Year-captain on the last world, had joined them at his own request only a few weeks ago, shiptime; he would never hold another official post aboard *Gypsy Moth.*

They found the Year-captain, Gilhart, and Gilrae, who was serving as Co-ordinator this year, in old Gilharrad's quarters. When Raban came in, it was the Elder, not the Captain, who immediately guessed their mission.

"The new planet's a good one."

"Looks like it," Raban said. "It was young Doran who found it, though, and checked it out, so that credit really belongs to him."

The captain, Gilhart, a man (apparently) in the prime of life, short and thick-set for an Explorer, with broad heavy cheekbones and peculiarly deep-set eyes, smiled in a friendly way, and said "Good work, youngster. It's about time."

"I've always thought Doran had an instinct for planet-finding," Gilrae said, with a warm smile. She came and laid her arm lightly around Gildoran's shoulder.

Gilhart scoffed "Is that a woman's intuition, Rae?" It sounded like an old joke between them, and Gildoran went stiff under Rae's arm.

"It's not a joke," old Gilharrad said, "I've often thought planet-finding is an instinct. A survival skill for Explorers, maybe. A psychic talent that some people have, like perfect pitch. Oh, yes, you young people can scoff all you like, but in my time more planets have been found by instinct and hunch than by all your scientific computations, Hart."

"I'll have to take your word for it," Gilhart chuckled, "because if it's a talent, I'm evidently tone-deaf. I trust my instruments."

"And much good they were doing you," Gilrae said affectionately. "Three years since the last good planet—I've been seeing frozen methane planets in my *sleep!*"

Gildoran watched the woman jealously.

She and Giltallen were paired before I was born. Now she's forgotten him and she's with Gilhart all the time.

He looked away from her, confused and angry as if she could read his thoughts.

Gilharrad said "Perhaps the planet simply was not ready to be found."

Gildoran looked at the old man. His wrinkled face was peaceful, his eyes half-closed; his body, fragile and emaciated until the old bones barely seemed enclosed by the flesh, lay supported in a flotation hammock; he was smiling a little. The young man said uncertainly "You're joking, of course."

"No. Perhaps the planet called to us unconsciously, and we reacted without knowing it. After all, what do we know of worlds, our own brains are only magnetic fields, and planets have enormous magnetic fields. Why should one magnetic field not tune in to another?"

It makes a strange kind of sense. From where he is now, who knows what he sees?

Gilrae said softly "Planets have a call. Every now and then someone will feel that call, and leave the Ships for some particular world . . . like Giltallen. . . ."

Gilhart said in a low voice "There used to be a saying: "For every Explorer, somewhere there's a world with his name on it!"

Gilharrad said peacefully, "If that were true, then mine must be somewhere outside Cosmos, for now I will die as I lived, here on the *Gypsy Moth.*"

The Captain grimaced. "Well, this one's waiting. Let's hope it doesn't have anyone's name on it; we're short-handed."

The Elder smiled, a smile of utter content and peace. He said "Well, go along, you children, and look at your new world. You young people are always excited about every new planet!"

"Well, it's our job," Gilhart said.

Gilharrad shrugged that off. "Planets! Planets are only holes in space! They are only interruptions in the true Cosmos!"

"They're what the Explorers are all about," Gilhart said, and Gilharrad shook his frail head. "You think so? Never mind, some day the time will come when you can see the truth. Our true purpose is only the quest, the seeking. The planets are only the excuse." His eyes dropped over his lids wearily. "I will meditate on this new world and see what place it has within the completeness of the Cosmos," he sighed, and immediately he slept.

The others quietly left the low-gravity room, and only when they were outside in the shaft did Gilhart say "I wonder if he means all that stuff, or if he's playing a straight-faced joke on us all? I hate to think his mind's cracking."

Gilrae shrugged. "Who's to say what's true?"

Gilhart said "Well, it's too mystic for me. I take it you're still excited about landing, Rae?"

The woman smiled. "Not really. I just get caught up in subjective time and meditation, and then I have to come down into gravity routines again. I can never meditate properly when we're downworlding."

Raban said sourly "Shall I fix you up a place in the Floaters level, Rae? Not *this* year, please. We're too short-handed."

She shook her head and her bleached hair went flying in the low gravity. Again it seemed to Gildoran that she had not changed a particle since he was in Nursery; he wondered how old she was, and felt a stab of pain at the thought of her changing, however little.

How old is she, anyway? You never knew, unless the person was younger than you.

"Don't mind me," Gilrae said, "I'm not due for Floater status for another hundred years shiptime. At least. Maybe three hundred. It's just . . . oh, well, life would be perfect if we didn't have to work for a living. I used to think of space as just something we had to get through between planets. Now it's the other way around. So let's go get through with it, and we'll never do that till we start."

Down on the Nursery level, the children were being

tucked into hammocks by the great slow-moving Pooh-bears; when Gildoran came in, one of them broke off and came toward him.

"Is there news, Gildoran?"

"Yes. A planet," he said, "nickel-iron core, so we're going in tomorrow."

The great brown-furred alien smiled with relief. "I was afraid we'd have to try synthesizing it," she said. "Three of the babies are showing signs of primary anemia. Now, of course, there's no hurry. Do you want to come in and say good night, Gildoran?"

He stepped into the great room, where the four three-year-olds who had survived after the last liftoff were being tucked into their hammocks, and a small group of six-year-olds were eating supper. The six-year-olds were already bleached like Explorers; skin translucently white, hair silvery pale; but the four small heads on the pillows of their hammocks were still dark-brown, rust-colored, blonde. One of them wriggled loose and came running, naked, to Gildoran, squealing his name. He bent and lifted her up, hugging the tiny girl close. She was the little one with the long almond-tilted eyes, her cheeks round and rosy. In her hand she jingled a tiny pair of castanets with rhythmic insistence.

"I want to play for you," she demanded.

"But it's bedtime, Small," he said indulgently, "another time."

"Then *you* tuck me in. No, go away, naughty Pooh," said the child, frowning and striking out at the Poohbear who came to take her from Gildoran, "Not love you. Love Gildoran."

Ramie, supervising the six-year-olds in handling their spoons, looked up, stifling laughter. "You have a fatal charm, Gildoran."

The Poohbear said staidly "You needn't bother with her unless you wish, Gildoran."

"No, I'll tuck her in," he said, bending over and deftly sliding the tiny girl into her hammock. This was his special charge from that long-ago shift of nursery duty, one of the six he had Transmitted from the Hatchery. During the long period of anxiety after the DNA operations which modified the babies to survive in space, he had been the one to watch over her nights, listening to her breathing, suffering with her in the weariness of her long convalescence. Two of the six had died, but this one had lived. Gildoran's had been the first face she recognized when she was six months old; and it was he who had sought and received permission to name her Gilmarina, after his old playmate, lost in riots off Lasselli's World. He bent now, and kissed the small, rosy, charming face, saying severely as he could manage "Go to sleep now, Marina, and you shall play your castanets for me another time.

I had a hunch she'd be musical.

Secretly, for no one ever would say it aloud, he thought that he knew, just a little, what it must be like to be a father.

I wonder if that's why every one of us—from the Captain to the twelve-years-olds—has to take a turn, every year, at Nursery duty? Just so we won't forget?

Ramie was finishing with the six-year-olds. She called to him lightly "Just a minute, Gildoran, I'm off-shift and we can go up together." Her smile told Gildoran how pleased she was at the prospect. He squirmed. But what could he do? They had to live together on the *Gypsy*

Moth, maybe for hundreds of years. He wasn't in love with her. He loved her, but only as he loved all of them, all people who had always been there. But he couldn't rebuff her, make trouble, cause misery. He waited.

Watching the Poohbears, he felt—for the hundredth time—curious about these aliens who lived among the Explorers without being *of* them. They had always been there. But why? What did they derive from their contact with the Explorers?

It's necessary, of course. Every one of us—we live so long—is a potential sexual mate for every other Explorer. With the Poohbears for our mothers, we avoid any maternal relationship. Therefore there's never a hint of incest.

But where did the Poohbears come from? Did anyone even know?

He stared at the enigmatic, furred, beloved face of the Poohbear who had come to adjust Gilmarina's covers around her small bare shoulders, with a wave of old, habitual love and affection. But he realized that he did not even know the Poohbear's personal name, or even if she had one. Or even, he thought with sudden shock, if she were a *she!* Somehow the speculation felt wrong, and he supposed one didn't speculate about one's mother's sexuality.

But Poohbear isn't even my own species! Yet she's my mother. Crazy!

Ramie came up to him, jauntily slipping her arm through his. "I'm finished. Let's go up to the Bridge, Gildoran, I want to look at the new planet. I expect I'll be baby-sitting most of the time we're here, but I can *look* at it, and hope there's enough sun to give the babies sun-baths."

"Are you disappointed that you're on Nursery duty while we're downworlding this time?"

"I don't know," she said, "maybe I'd hoped to be on Transmitter detail. It's exciting to hook it up the first time and feel that you're tying a new world into a network of a hundred thousand worlds. But there'll be other planets, and I'm sure to hit Transmitter detail on one of them sooner or later. There's plenty of time."

"I wish I could be that contented about things."

Damn. There are so many good things about Ramie. I hate feeling at odds with her this way.

She glanced at him sidelong out of her strangely tilted dark eyes, and said quietly "I'm not always that content-ed, Gildoran. I just don't like to get hysterical about things I can't change. That doesn't mean I'm just . . . ac-cepting them. I don't suppose you've changed your mind?"

"No," he said, "I haven't changed my mind, Ramie."

Her voice sounded a little bitter. She said "Well, I sup-pose there's time for that too."

He made his voice hard. "Don't count on it."

She tightened her hand briefly on his wrist. She said "Gildoran, I swear I won't be angry or . . . or make jeal-ous scenes, but . . . is it Lori you want?"

He flared in real anger "That's not worthy of you! Lori's just a baby. What do you think I am?"

"As I remember, she made Class B a few weeks ago shiptime. I seem to remember you and poor Gilmarin being very indignant when someone spoke of *our* group as children, during that time. And you've spent all your time with her for the last year."

Gildoran pointed out with restraint that he had been teaching Gillori to operate the Communications Desk during duty hours, and was not given to spending his recreation time with little children unless he was on Nursery duty. "You might as well be jealous of Gilmarina—I spend more time with her than I do with Lori, off duty."

Gilramie sighed. She said "It isn't jealousy, exactly, Doran. It's just . . ." she made a helpless gesture, "oh, call it habit, I'm used to you, maybe I simply haven't the . . . oh, the inner strength to take up with someone else. Maybe I'm just following the line of least resistence. If I knew, positively, that you cared for someone else maybe it would be easier."

Gildoran felt intensely sorry for her, but even through his pity there was enough resentment to turn away without answering. Ramie sighed and said "Oh, all right, forget I said anything. Pure self-indulgence on my part. Let's go along and have a look at the new planet."

II

There were twelve in the small shuttle ship which always went down first; that was the minimum number to do the basic, preliminary work without leaving the ship short-handed. This was always the one real point of danger, the first penetration of a completely unknown planet. As they dropped through the thick cloud-cover, Gildoran felt his muscles tensing with a curious, cold, strangely bracing fear. It was the first time he'd drawn landing-party duty, but he'd heard plenty about what you could find on a really strange planet. When he was still in the Nursery, four members of a landing-party had gone into an innocent-looking, deserted swamp; within two minutes, all four had been swooped on, and literally chewed up by swift-flying carnivorous birds. There had not even been enough left of them to bury.

Tradition required the Year-Captain to lead every landing party. It was the only way to divide this dangerous duty with absolute fairness; the Year-Captains were chosen by lot, and everyone on shipboard over twenty-one was eligible, unless he or she had been Year-Captain within the past ten years. Gilhart was up front next to old Gildorric, who was navigating; the other members of the landing party had been chosen either because there was a need for the specialty they were filling this year— or because they were junior enough to be expendable. Gildoran knew he still came into that category, and so did Gillori, who was wedged into the seat beside him, chattering from sheer nervousness. One of the Poohbears was among the crew to check the suitability of the climate for the children; if it was doubtful they would be kept inside the *Gypsy Moth*, if it was healthful, an outdoor camp would be set up immediately so that the children could get accustomed, again, to gravity and sunlight.

Lori said "What would happen if there was already an Explorer ship down there?"

Gilrae looked back at the girl and said "It's been known to happen. About thirty years ago we teamed up with the *Tinkerbelle*, opening a big system with three habitable planets. But none of our signals were answered from space this time, so no Explorers. It's all ours." She frowned faintly, and Gilhart, looking over her shoulder at her instruments, said "What's the matter, Rae? Something not looking quite right?"

She shook her head. "Nothing I can put a finger on. Maybe it looks *too* good, maybe I'm wondering why no one's picked this one yet."

"Law of averages," said Gilhart with his winning grin. "We've got to have some luck. Don't go psychic on us, darling. If you do feel psychic, save it for . . . let's say . . . a more personal occasion." He laid a hand on the nape of her neck, and the woman smiled up at him, still bent over her controls, reaching her free hand up to take his.

Gildoran looked away.

The hell of it is, you can't even have the satisfaction of not liking Gilhart. He's such a damn nice fellow. You can even see what Rae sees in him. Everybody likes him.

It was a relief to hear Lori start chattering again. Lori

asked "What happens if we run out of planets some day?"

"We're in trouble," Gildoran said lightly, then more seriously "But it's not possible. That's a big, big Universe out there, Gillori. Even if only one star in a thousand had planets, and only one planet in a thousand was habitable, we still could go on for a million million years without exhausting the Galaxy, and that's just this *one* Galaxy."

"It's like the old story of the Marching Chinese." Gilhart said, "and don't ask me what the Chinese were because I never knew, but there used to be an old story that you could never line 'em up and count them because there were so many billions that by the time you came to the end of the line a whole new generation was born, grown up and having more children. Maybe they were some kind of rabbits. Anyway, by the time we came— theoretically—to the end of all the planets which exist *now*, more stars and planets would have evolved and cooled down and more spiral nebulae would have been thrown off and so forth. Of course, none of us would live that long—probably not even the oldest Floater still alive in the fleet—but theoretically, at least, the Explorers could go on for eternity."

"Now who's getting mystical?" Gilrae laughed. "Dorric, do you have the coordinates from meteorology? Where are we going to set down?"

"Off the equator," the navigator replied, "Southern hemisphere, fairly near the seashore but far enough inland to avoid coastal rainfall belts. I don't much like the wind patterns in the Northern hemisphere; too much danger of setting down in a hurricane belt, unless we could wait out a full season and observe. I can't guarantee anything, but this area should have as good a climate as we're likely to find."

"Not too cold, I hope for the children's sake," the Poohbear said in her gentle voice.

"I'll put in a special requisition," Gilrae said.

Gradually the small landing craft dropped down toward the cloud cover. There was the unfamiliar sensation of weight growing as they came within the gravitational field and slackened speed, so that they were no longer an object in free orbit, but a vehicle with a described, not an orbital path above the planet. The brilliant sunlight dimmed and became vapory and translucent as they went into the thick clouds.

"With this much cloud cover we might get a greenhouse effect," said the second-string botanist, Gilmerritt, "Once we get this planet opened up it might turn out to be a health resort."

"Congratulations," Gilhart said absently, "you have just won the long-distance conclusion-jump award. Planet not even landed on, and you're building a health resort."

"I'm not superstitious," Gilmerritt said with a touch of defensiveness, "We've done enough preliminary checking from space to know it's habitable, and that was an educated guess based on my experience in my own specialty."

Gilhart swung around to look at her. His face was very grave. He said "There's only so much checking we can do from space. Even if the last fifteen planets have been perfect—or the last *hundred*—never forget; there is no single planet in the Universe that's like any other. Maybe ninety-nine in a hundred that look good enough to land on could be playgrounds, health resorts, what have you. But sooner or later you're going to land on one that bites back."

"You really are accentuating negative thinking, aren't you, Captain?" Merritt said, a little startled.

He shook his head. "Always hope for the best," he

said, "but don't *expect* it. Because that's when Explorers get taken off guard. And, sometimes, when they get killed. Okay, everybody, end of lecture. There are twelve of us landing. I'd like twelve of us to go home again tonight, if you're all agreeable, so pay attention. . . . Dorric; ready to land?"

"Ready, Captain," he confirmed.

"Cut in the atmospherics, and take us down."

The atmospheric drives came in with a roar, and conversation became impossible in the landing craft cabin. Gildoran, yawning to ease the build-up of pressure inside his ears, felt the tension, briefly dispelled by the good-natured banter, build up again.

His planet.

He had discovered it. To some extent he would always be identified, in the minds of the crew of the *Gypsy Moth*, with this world. It was just one of those things. Not in the rules, of course. Legally it was the Captain's responsibility, and the Science Officer's, to decide whether or not it was a good world, one they could open and lock into the chain of the Transmitter. In the eyes of the galaxy, the success or failure of this world belonged not to any one man, but to the Explorers as a whole in general, and to the *Gypsy Moth* in particular.

Legally, and according to ship's rules, Gildoran would get no credit if the planet turned out well, and no blame if it turned out badly.

But it was one of those things. In the minds of the *Gypsy Moth's* crew, it was Gildoran's world, and if it was a good world it would somehow add to his stature and his reputation. And if it turned out to be a catastrophe—well, legally they couldn't fault him, they couldn't penalize him, it was just bad luck, but they wouldn't forget. Not in thirty years of shiptime, not in a hundred years, they wouldn't forget.

He raised his head, blinking with the strain of the descent, and stared at the rapidly growing image of the green world below them.

His world.

The whine of the atmospherics grew to a scream; then diminished. Instead of plunging through atmosphere, they were floating quietly, in the landing craft; hovering above what seemed to be a flat and featureless sea of green.

Gildorric asked "Do we burn off a space to set down, Captain?"

Gilhart shook his head. "Not right away. We will if we have to, but do a skim at a few hundred feet. Find an open space, if you can. Seems a shame to burn up any of that nice forest, and then we have to start controlling the fires right away. Not to mention the damage to any animal life. A burnoff should be a last resort. Not to mention that if we set down in the middle of a jungle, it's hardly a good spot for a Transmitter."

Rae chuckled. "I remember once when we had to set a 24-hour guard over our equipment for six weeks while we were building. Turn your back for half a second and the small tools and wire just weren't there. Things like monkeys in the forest would snatch them up and we'd find them in the mud a few hours later—I think the little beasties used them for toys. It was maddening."

Gildorric grinned and said "I think *you* were still in the Nursery, Rae, when we landed on a world where there were insects who grabbed our wire and chewed it up—and digested it, too. Did we ever have fun getting the first Transmitter up on *that* place!"

Lori asked "But you *did* get it set up? Do you *always* get it set up?"

Gilhart shook his head slowly. "No. Like I say, sometimes you hit a world that bites back, and then all you can do is run. If you've got anything left to run *with*."

"Don't frighten the children," Gildorric said genially, "that doesn't happen twice in a lifetime. Come here, Hart, and take a look through the viewer. How does this spot at the edge of the lake strike you? We'd have water supply for the camp, and it's grassy edge—plenty of solid ground."

Gilhart poised over the great flat table-like screen where a projection of the ground surface was visible. "You mean the spot in the lee of those cliffs?"

"More or less. Out on the grasslands, where there doesn't seem to be too much underbrush," Gildorric said. "Those dark masses are some kind of plant, but not so big we can't get through. We can test for bedrock, and if it's solid enough, set up the Transmitter under the cliff somewhere."

Gilhart nodded slowly. "I suppose so. And if not, we could camp here while we explore for a better site. All right, take us down to the surface. And try not to land us in a swamp."

The landing craft slowly descended; came to rest with a faint jolt. Gilhart and a couple of the older crew members were joking with Gildorric about the landing—"You've been in space too long, you've lost your downworld touch, banging us down like that!" Gildoran slowly unfastened his seat straps.

He was in a tearing impatience to get out, actually to stand on the surface of the new world, but there was still some time to wait, while Gilmerritt checked test samples and sensors.

"The atmosphere looked fine from a few hundred feet up. But we want to be very sure what's at the surface." A few minutes later she nodded. "Plenty of oxygen, and, as you'd expect with all those clouds and all that green stuff, a lot of water vapor in the air. But the temperature is all right, and nothing troublesome in the atmosphere, just the usual inert gasses. Little high in ozone, but not enough to give trouble."

Gildorric glanced at Gilhart, and the Captain nodded.

"Formal command," he said. "Unlock doors. Establish landing."

Raban stood up and moved toward the door. Gildoran felt like crowding behind him. Gilrae met Gildoran's eyes and smiled. She said "It's always a thrill. No matter how often you do it. This is it, Gildoran. It's yours. Enjoy it."

He wanted to say, Oh Rae, I love you, and kiss her, but he didn't; he simply grinned at her, feeling foolish. She reached out and touched his shoulder affectionately.

She thinks I'm a child.

"It's Gildoran's world. Let him touch down first."

III

The whine of the doors opening, a rush of cool sharply-scented air; a swift, overpowering impression of greenness. Greenness everywhere; even the sky, under its thick layer of cloud, seemed to reflect pale green light below. Gildoran moved slowly down the steps and took the first hard impression of weight and a curious, yielding texture beneath his feet. It felt strange after years of low weight and super-smooth metalled and plastic floors underfoot. Now he stood on spongy green moss or grass, green in a belt of thick lush green of every hue. A green world, a greenish sky, the glimmer of green water in the distance somewhere.

He heard the other coming down the steps behind him. Gilmerritt sniffed audibly and said, "What did I say about greenhouse effect?"

It did smell strange. Was it the smell of the unknown vegetation all around, or was it simply that any air would have smelled strange after the chemically pure recycled air aboard *Gypsy Moth?*

The small landing craft was backed against a low cliff of some reddish stone, the only note of relief for the eyes against the green that otherwise was everywhere. The cliff stretched for nearly a mile, and sloped downward toward a small green lake, its surface just ruffled by a light wind. On the far shore of the lake a tall forest grew. Between the landing craft and the near shore of the lake stretched a wide green expanse of grassland, dotted here and there with thick clumps of bushlike growth; the cliff was lined with them, too. The nearer bushes were about five feet tall, with thick greyish branches and broad cup-shaped leaves; at the ends of the branches were cup-shaped flowers with a sunlit glitter.

It was very quiet except for the soft humming and chirping of insects which hopped in the grass, hovered over the flowers, and over the cup-shaped bushes. But so far there was nothing larger than an inch or so, except for one pale butterfly which seemed to like hovering over the cup-shaped blossoms. Gilmerritt walked toward the bushes; a trained biologist, she did not touch them, and would not until she was wearing thick plastic gloves—every Explorer biologist knew about the planets with fluoride-secreting flowers—but looked down at cup-shaped flower and butterfly with a pleased smile.

"Judging by looks, it still *looks* like a good place for a resort," she said. "Let's get started checking it out. I can hardly wait to see a luxury hotel here and people coming by Transmitter all across the Galaxy."

She laughed to show that she wasn't *really* jumping to conclusions this time. Gildoran thought nothing they built here could ever be as beautiful as the long expanse of green bush against the red granite and limestone of the cliffs, but he turned to Gilhart for orders.

"First step," Gilhart said, "put somebody on watch. Raban?"

The stocky older man nodded.

"Take somebody particularly able-bodied—Gilbarni, you care to go along?—draw two hand weapons from supplies, and climb up on the cliffs to keep watch for predators. Standing orders apply; don't shoot unless something obviously unintelligent looks as if it was going to attack anyone working down here. Station one man

71

down by the lake and between you, you can cover the whole landing party." .

"Right." Raban and young Barni stepped back into the landing craft; emerged with hand weapons and gloves, and began to move along the foot of the cliff looking for a good spot to climb.

"Rae, did you say this was glacial moraine?" Gilhart asked.

"That's right," Rae said, shading her eyes against the light, "There should be good solid bedrock underneath; it might serve as a location for the first Transmitter set-up, although it's going to take a couple of weeks study to be sure. The first step is to get some core samples—here and down by the lake."

The Captain nodded. "Gildoran, you and Lori can work the core sampler. Gilmerritt, you take everybody else but Gilrae and start getting soil, water and life samples. Be sure everybody knows about wearing gloves, too. And Gilrae, you work with Poohbear, hunting for a good place for a Nursery camp. You know the kind of terrain we need."

She nodded. "Yes. And may I say something, Captain?" They were all being formal now; they were on the job. Gilhart nodded for permission, and Rae said "All of you. Don't forget we need a good, solid spot to set down *Gypsy Moth*, so don't ignore any possibilities. The place we had on the last world—everyone except Lori probably remembers—was just about perfect. It was backed up against a mountain, and we didn't have to move it until we were ready for liftoff again. But I'm sure all of you remember the trouble we had with mud, so try to look for a spot where we can put in hard-surfaced walkways without too many extra man-hours. That's about all. Captain? Anything else?"

"Just that we'll break for a meal in four hours shiptime.

72

Daylight here lasts eighteen hours, so we may have trouble judging time by sunlight."

They scattered to their various tasks; it took Gildoran and Lori the best part of an hour to unload the core sampling tool, and assemble it with the compact battery generators and the wheeled drive for moving it around.

"Clumsy thing," Lori grumbled, and Gildoran laughed. "Rae told me when she was a kid core-sampling drills had to be moved around on a truck. It was less than two hundred years ago that somebody on Vega 14 developed a hand-wheeled one. We can do as much in three days as it once took Gilharrad six weeks shiptime to do on a new planet, poor old chap. And we don't have to wait and carry all this stuff up to *Gypsy Moth* to test it, now that we have the groundlab facilities in the landing craft. There's a complete biological and geological laboratory—well, not complete, but complete enough for preliminary work—right here in the landing craft."

The girl shaded her eyes with her hand. "Doran, are there any eyeshades or protectors in the landing craft?"

"I don't know. The light isn't that bad, is it? What's the matter, Lori?"

"Glare, or something. I'm getting a wretched headache."

Gildoran, now that he came to notice it, had a headache himself. "Maybe it's just gravity," he hazarded, "when we're not used to it. You can ask somebody, I guess."

"No, it's not worth bothering, I'll ask Pooh when we break for lunch." She tightened a screw bolt on the sampling tool, and gave it a shove with her hand. "There, I guess it'll run all right if the grass isn't too thick, or these little hoppers don't get inside and jam the wheels."

"There certainly are a lot of insects around," Gildoran agreed. He picked one carefully off his uniform.

"Now what?"

"Run it down by the lake, I guess, and wait until somebody gets enough water samples to be sure first, that what's in the lake is really water, and second, that it will work in our drilling fluid—not too many chemicals that could dissolve the bit or clog it up."

Lori looked at him quizzically. "And what if it *isn't* water, or it's full of dissolved borax or something?"

"Then," Gildoran said, "you can personally have the fun of going into the groundlab and *distilling* a few thousand gallons for us, sweet. Fortunately it doesn't have to be pure enough to drink in order to keep the drill bit cool. But every so often you run into some lake full of sulphuric acid, or some such thing."

Lori wrinkled up her childish face in disgust. "If that lake's full of sulphuric acid, this is no place for a landing camp . . . I think you're teasing me, Gildoran."

"Well, maybe just a little bit. They did a lot of the preliminary checking in the geodesic studies from *Gypsy Moth*, in orbit. And most of what's in the atmosphere is just plain water vapor, period, so that's probably what we'll find in the lakes and the oceans and the rivers too."

"So we go down to the lake?"

"Why bother? Gilmerritt or one of her crew will be up pretty soon with the first crop of samples, and she knows we need water for the drilling fluid. Let's hope we're lucky; if it's water, and even halfway pure, all we need is a good long supply of hose, a mixing pump, and we're all ready to go."

It was not long until Gildorric, bearing the early samples, came up from the lake, and reported that the water was just water, and rather exceptionally pure. "There's a lot of water-weed in it, so it might not be much good as a swimming-pool," he reported, "but it'll run your drill bits, and it's good to drink—very good. Trace minerals, but nothing much except limestone, in any quantity, and that's wholesome enough. So you children can rig up your hoses and pumps, and get working on the samples."

The machinery was automatic; once Gildoran and Lori had rigged up their tool and chosen a spot for the first sample, there was nothing to do except check the gauges every few minutes to make certain that the bit remained vertical and the hoses containing the drilling fluid did not clog, and they could sit back and watch the others moving around near the edge of the lake, collecting samples, returning to the landing craft groundlab to test them. When the first core samples came up from the drill, Gildoran examined them quickly for porosity and obvious rock types, then put them aside—they would be more extensively tested aboard *Gypsy Moth.*

Lori said, "I still don't understand why we can't have a Transmitter inside the landingcraft and send samples up that way, after we've landed. The *Gypsy Moth* is up here, and we could bring a Transmitter down——"

"Go back to First Grade, Lori. The *Gypsy Moth* is in orbit—not just *hanging* there. We can't Transmit to a moving target."

"But everything in the Universe is moving, isn't it? Yet every planet has nine or ten Transmitters——"

"Yes. But one of the things we do here is plot the regular orbital motion of this planet around its sun, and this sun around its position in the Galaxy, and that's all programmed into the Transmitter, so it knows *exactly* where in the Galaxy we'll be at any given miscrosecond for the next million years. That information goes to Head Centre, and the nineteen or twenty backup Centres, in case Head Centre goes out of contact or its star goes Nova, perish the thought."

They had a sizable group of core samples by the time
Gildoran's chronometer told him it was time to assemble
for meal break. Field rations had been brought down
and they gathered in the shade of the landingcraft for
their food; the ground was soft and spongy beneath their
bodies.

Gilmerritt took off her slippers and wriggled her toes
in the grass; Gildoran reached out and touched the soft
skin of her foot; it was plump and smooth and pretty.
Gilmerritt leaned against him and murmured "Was that
an invitation, Gildoran?"

"It's whatever you want to make it."

She said teasingly "I thought you had everything all
set up with Ramie."

"That's what everyone thinks, and I'm getting slightly
weary of it," Gildoran said. He looked across to where
the Captain and Rae, slightly apart from the rest of the
crew, had their heads close together.

*Rae's out of my reach and I'm damned if I'll pair off
with Ramie because that's what everybody expects.*

Merritt looked up at him. She was a pretty, round-
faced woman with eyes of lustrous green, and a faintly
cleft chin with deep dimples. "There's something about a
planet," she murmured teasingly. "I can live solitary for
months at a time in deep space but no sooner do we go
downworlding than I start remembering that I'm a
woman, and looking sidewise at all of you."

He caressed the plump toes of her foot, the soft well-
manicured nails. Then, reluctantly, he said "I think you
probably ought to put your slippers on again, Merritt.
The soil hasn't been tested——"

"And it might be full of sub-microscopic hookworms
and parasites that have an affinity for human skin. I'm

sure you're right," Merritt said reluctantly, and pulled on her silvery sandals. As she fastened the straps she murmured "Don't look now, but I'm getting some very nasty glances from little Gillori. It's your fatal charm, Gildoran."

Gildoran felt a spasm of anger. Lori was getting entirely too possessive. Knowing that the child's eyes were on him, he leaned over and kissed Merritt, long and slow and very thoroughly.

When they came apart she sighed. "I've wanted to do that for some time. But on the last planet you were all wrapped up in some earthworm girl. . . ."

With a sudden start Gildoran realized he had not thought of Janni in years. "That was strictly a downworld thing," he said lightly, and kissed her again, before Gilhart and Rae came strolling over from the lee of the cliff.

"Shall I call Raban down for dinner?" one of the crew asked. "They could come one at a time."

"No, let them stay on watch, but take them some food," Gilhart commanded. He passed a hand over his head, scowling. "Are you *sure* they tested the air before landing, Rae? No, no, nothing to eat, Gildorric, I feel as if I'd been poisoned."

Gilrae said slowly "The air's fine. A little high in ozone until we get used to it, but nothing we can't adapt to—" she broke off. "Lori! Sweetheart, what's the matter?"

The young girl said in a wavering voice "Sorry, I . . . I think I'm going to be sick—" and promptly was. Gilmerritt scrambled to her feet and hurried to attend her; Lori tried to push her away for a moment, then was content to rest against the older woman's shoulder. Rae went to bend over her. Gildoran said "She was complaining of headache earlier, said it was the glare."

Rae said "It doesn't seem that bright. How do the rest of you feel?"

"Headache," said Gildoran, and the Captain nodded. "Me too—rotten one."

"It's no wonder," said the Poohbear with sudden violence, "this world is so damned *noisy!*"

Eleven faces turned to her in startlement; Lori did not raise her head but lay limply against Merritt's breast. Gilhart said "Take her inside the landingcraft, Merritt. Can you walk, Lori, or do you want Doran to carry you?"

"I can walk," the child said, struggling to her feet, but she let Gilmerritt support her with an arm round her waist. Gilhart said to Poohbear "I'm surprised, Pooh. Noisy? It seems quiet to me. I don't hear a thing, except the insects humming. Any of you?"

"I suppose it could be the insects," said the brown-furred alien, with a deprecating smile. Her eyes looked strained. "Buzz, chirp, drone, hum, I just don't like it."

"And some of us have headaches," Gilhart said. "It can't be the air, we sampled all that very carefully, and tested for any known disease organism."

Rae said "The headaches could be from the ozone, of course. They probably are. We'll get used to that, but it could take a couple of days. How are the samples looking?"

"Good so far," said Gildorric. "Merritt's with Lori, so I'll report. The water's good, the soil seems good enough and fertile enough—if it grows all this stuff, it'll certainly grow food plants. There are nuts and berries which might test out as edible vegetable protein—and the plants are certainly hardy. So far none of them test out poisonous, either, and none of the insects are any bigger than a hopper."

"Animal life?" Gilhart asked.

"So far, none. We should check the other continents when we get some surface travel down, but so far, so good. As far as I know we could go ahead with the Transmitter tonight, but of course we need to make some more extensive tests. Just to make sure there are no hidden jokers like viruses."

So far, so good, Gildoran thought; his world was testing out almost too good to be true. Then why did he feel so flat, so let-down, so miserable? Had his expectations been too high? Was it just reaction from being keyed-up over the new world? It was a good world, even a beautiful one.

Gilrae asked "How soon can we get the children down, Pooh? We found a perfect spot for the Nursery camp."

The Poohbear looked strained, almost haggard.

"I don't like it," she said slowly. 'I know I'm being irrational, but I somehow don't feel right about bringing the children down into a place like this."

"It's up to you, of course," Gilrae said; "You and the other Poohbears are in charge of the children. But after all, it was you, Pooh, who reminded me that some of them were showing iron deficiency and were in a hurry to get them down."

"I know. As I said, I know I'm being irrational," the Poohbear said, "but I still can't see it. Couldn't we give them land-based drinking water—it has a good iron content—for a few days until you finish the tests?"

Gilhart frowned. "I'd be inclined to trust your instinct, Pooh," he said. "Let's leave it at that. Collect some land-based water—the lake water will do—and possibly some iron ore to feed into the ship's supplies of chemicals. Keep the children on board until we're sure."

She smiled at him with relief. "Thank you, Hart. That would relieve my mind." Gildoran reflected that probably the Poohbear was the only person on board the Explorer ship who called the Captain simply "Hart." Except perhaps Rae, in private.

The Poohbear said "And if that's settled, why not let me go inside the landingcraft, and look after Lori? My ears can't take the noise, and it will release Merritt to finish her sampling for the day."

A light wind was rising as the Poohbear swung her heavy, furry body up the landingcraft steps. Gildorric said "I wonder what she's worried about?"

"Who can say?" Gilhart was struggling to keep his loose notes together. "Probably their hearing is in a different range than ours. Human hearing is relatively dull —only from 15 cycles-per-second up to twenty thousand or so. Sounds have been measured up to two million cps or so."

Gildoran was reminded again how little they knew about the Poohbears. Well, maybe everyone needed a touch of mystery. As if this new planet wasn't mystery enough!

Gilmerritt, returning, commented that Lori was still feeling deathly sick and that the Poohbear was looking after her. Before she went off to her work she looked with a long smile at Gildoran, and he returned it.

The Captain said "With Lori out of commission, you'll need someone to help you, Doran. Gildorric?"

"Anyone who knows how to run a core sampler."

Gildorric chuckled. "I was running a core sampler while the planet you came from was going through the Stone Age, Doran. Let's go."

Gilhart swore, testily. "Damn this wind! I'm going to move my things over in the lee of the cliff there. Those bushes should break the wind, and I can spread out the geodesic plots for this area. Can you give me a hand with this stuff before we go back to work, somebody? Rae, send up some food for the men on the cliff. And make sure the sun isn't getting to them; there isn't much shade up there."

That's what it is to be a Captain, Gildoran thought. He himself would have forgotten the guards on the cliffs, but Gilhart had remembered. He had to remember everything.

All that afternoon Gildoran worked with the core sampler, at Gildorric's side. They took samples beneath the cliff, near the lake shore, and finally walked around to the far side of the lake, testing the depth of the soil and the depth of the bedrock. Finally, as the light was beginning to lessen, they wound up the hoses and dried the pump, wheeling their sampling tool back near the landingcraft.

"Good firm bedrock everywhere near here," Gildorric said. "We can probably set the *Gypsy Moth* down below the cliffs, and establish our base here, provided everything else tests out properly. We'll need to start the mining machinery, but back in the hills there should be plenty of metals. It's a good, rich planet. Merritt's a fool; this place is too good to waste on a resort hotel."

"It's natural for her to think in terms of her own specialty," Gildoran defended.

Gildorric laughed. "And she's a pretty woman—I saw you flirting with her."

Gildoran had sense enough to ask amiably "Not jealous, are you?" instead of flaring up.

"Jealous? Act your age, boy," Gildorric said, "I've known Merritt most of my life and we've worked together so many years you wouldn't believe it. But I guess we known each other too well. Let's face it, when you're my age you know *all* the woman aboard the *Gypsy Moth* too well. Which is why . . ." he chuckled again, "I'm really getting excited about having the Transmitter set up again, and being in contact with the Galaxy. Just the fact of seeing a few new faces. Don't mistake me," he cautioned, "I'm not saying I don't love Merritt. I'd die for her—as I would for any of you," he added in a moment of complete seriousness. "But she just doesn't excite me any more. It's been a long cruise. You're probably too young to know what I mean, but when you've been paired at least three times with every woman on the crew, and even made a few offbeat trips with the men, you'll know why most of us save our romance—and our sex—for downworlding."

Is that why Ramie doesn't excite me, I know her too well?

They were near the landingcraft now, and other members of the landing party were bringing back their equipment and their samples, getting ready to board. It was Gilmerritt who noticed that the Captain had not yet returned. She went to Rae, as second in command, to ask "Have the guards been called in yet? There's no need to keep Gilraban and Barni up there in the broiling sun now that we're all in."

"That's for Gilhart to say," Rae returned, "but I see no harm in sending for them to come down. You attend to it, Merritt. Gildoran, have *you* seen the Captain?"

It was Gildorric who answered, "No, neither of us have seen him since lunchtime, but he moved his plots and papers over in the lee of the cliff where the wind wouldn't be getting at them. Want me to go give him a hand with them?"

"You've got the atmospherics to handle," Rae said, "Let Gildoran go. Doran—and tell him I ordered the guards in, will you?"

Gildoran went off in the direction he had last seen Gilhart moving, toward the cliff lined with tall bushes and their green cup-shaped blossoms. The sun was lowering now, and the clouds thickening so that the light had diminished somewhat, but the cup-flowers still seemed to glimmer by some inner light. There was no sign of Gilhart, and Gildoran, puzzled, began to walk along the lower edge of the cliff, his eyes alert, his head turning from side to side for any trace of the Captain. He felt a strange unease that was almost tangible, like a nasty taste in his mouth. After he had walked a few hundred feet along the cliff, and seen nothing but the green-grey branches and translucent cup-flowers, he began to be really worried. If it had been anyone on *Gypsy Moth* except the Captain, he would have shouted his name. And not too gently, either. His distress and worry were quickly mingled with anger; he could imagine what Gilhart would have to say if any of the crew had gone off like that.

In spite of shipboard etiquette he began to call.

"Gilhart! Gilhart! Captain!"

There was no answer; no sound at all, except for the constant humming of insects in the underbrush—how he was beginning to hate that sound!—and the soft rustle of the wind in the cups of the bushes.

Gildoran shouted, this time at the top of his considerable lungs;

"Captain! Captain!

Still the silence, broken only by the soft wind-rustle. Then Gildoran saw something which drew his glance quickly; a square of bluish-white, too regular, too bright to be any natural object in all this green, lying amid the cup-flowers. He pushed the branches aside. Thorns on the underbrush stung and lacerated his hands and snagged at his uniform; he put his hand in his mouth and sucked the bleeding fingers, but he thrust on, his heart pounding in sudden violent fear.

He found Gilhart lying in a small hollow between the plants and the red limestone of the cliff base, crumpled in a heap. Gildoran bent over him, angry and apprehensive. Lori had been sick and the Captain should have known he could get sick too, he shouldn't have gone off alone. How could anyone have heard him if he'd called for help? But against this angry interior monologue Gildoran was kneeling beside the fallen man, unfastening his tunic and thrusting his hand inside, helplessly hunting for a pulse. But he already knew that the Captain was dead.

IV

". . . So we can't go down again until we know what killed him," Gildoran finished, and Ramie's soft almond eyes looked gentle and miserable. "Oh, poor, poor Gilrae! They were so close, Gildoran, they've always been so close to each other. Is she all right?"

"As much as she can be, I suppose," Gildoran said, sombrely. He was haunted by the memory of Rae's drawn, haggard face, bloodless and wretched as she struggled to pull herself together. As second officer, she was in command of *Gypsy Moth* until a new Captain could be chosen; and though the laws of the Explorers stipulated that this should be done within three days shiptime, there were still those three days to get through.

He was silent, remembering the last stressful half hour of their stay on the green world; the harrowing task of carrying Gilhart aboard, made harder by the gruesome task of stripping him to search his clothes for some possible cause—poisonous insect or animal which might have bitten him and be concealed in them. It had fallen to Gildoran to help roll the Captain in a blanket and carry one end of the heavy lump of clay that had been Gilhart, aboard the landingcraft. It had been a silent, sad journey upward through the cloud cover to the *Gypsy Moth*. Gilrae had insisted on kneeling beside the blanket-wrapped body, trying to keep it from rolling about grotesquely; they had let her have her way. They had all been paralyzed by her grief, and all of them had shared it. Lori sobbed with her head in the Poohbear's lap; Gilmerritt clung to Gildoran's hand, subdued, her merry green eyes downcast, and Gildoran knew that the woman was thinking of how Gilhart had good-naturedly teased and reproved her on the trip down. How light-hearted they had been then, and how different this trip back was!

Damn this world! Damn it!

Gildoran spared Ramie all this except the briefest account, knowing she too was saddened. "I did my first Class B duty on the bridge when he was Navigator," she said, "and he was so good-natured and so kind, always teasing me, and ready with a joke. And last year I worked in Medic with him. I simply can't believe that he's dead. But he was pretty old, Doran, couldn't it be natural causes?"

"Of course it could have been. It probably was. But we have to know for certain."

While they waited for the news, they went up to the Floaters quarters, to break the news to old Gilharrad. The ancient Explorer heard of Gilhart's death with a touch of sadness, but he did not weep. He sighed deeply and said "Well, it cannot be helped. The planet simply held the appointed end of his destiny, that is all. I know he would have preferred to die in space, but after all, space and downworld are all part of the same great Cosmos."

Before his ethereal calm Gildoran was reluctant to broach his errand.

"We are desperately short-handed, Harrad. Rae has asked if you can return to duty for a little while."

The old man sighed. "Must I?" he asked plaintively,

"I've earned a rest, haven't I? I like it up here, with nothing to do but meditate on the Ultimate Cosmos."

Gildoran said gently "You have certainly deserved a rest, Harrad, but we need you. And after all—" he added, with a certain amount of guile, "Gilhart never had a chance at *his* rest."

Gilharrad sighed again, deeply. "Well, well, I suppose I must," he said, "but just until the little ones grow up to Class B, mind you. And I refuse to go on the Ship's Officer list, I absolutely refuse. I'll advise, I'll work, I'll administer, but I won't hold Major Office, never again."

"I'm sure they'll agree to that," Ramie said, and held the thin old hand in hers for a moment. Gilharrad's flesh looked almost translucent, so bleached and thin that the pink color of the pulsing blood inside the cells was clearly visible, and Gildoran was struck with compassion, but they were desperately short-handed. To lose Gilhart! And so soon after Giltallen and Gilmarin had been lost to them! A scant three years, even before the little ones grew old enough to take their places!

"Poor Hart," Gilharrad mused, easing himself out of his gravity-free hammock. Reluctantly he stood up, sighing as he resigned himself to the drag of gravity again. "I suppose we'd better go down and find out what killed him."

It was only on such occasions as this that the entire crew of *Gypsy Moth*—everyone, except for the babies in the Nursery and the very oldest Floaters up in the gravity-free levels—gathered together in one place. Gildoran took his seat and realized that the huge Assembly Lounge was almost half empty. What was the normal compenent of an Explorer Ship? The ideal number was supposed to be a hundred. Surreptitiously, Gildoran counted. Sixty-three. And three six-year-olds and four three-year-olds in the Nursery. And seven Poohbears.

I wonder what's the fewest we could work the ship with? What happens if we drop under that number?

Gildoran saw others looking around and guessed that they were secretly counting, too.

Gilrae came slowly through the crowd to the front of the lounge. She looked pale, and as if she hadn't slept since Gilhart's death. Gildoran fervently hoped they didn't make her do the autopsy. Then she turned to the second-string Medic, a girl named Gilnosta, and took a memorandum from her, and Gildoran knew with relief that at least Rae had been spared *that*. It was about all she'd been spared, but she'd been spared that. It would have been hard enough for anyone. But worst for Rae.

Rae, Rae, what can I do to help you? What can I do to let you know how much I love you, how much I care for you, want to help you?

They didn't wait for Gilrae to call them to order. At her first breath there was complete quiet in the room. Her voice was low and strained.

"The autopsy reports on Gilhart show that he died of natural causes."

Of course, thought Gildoran. It had to be. He wasn't attacked by anything. There were no poisonous insects or reptiles near. Ozone isn't poisonous enough to kill.

Gilrae went on; "The circumstances are, we admit, a little confusing. There seem no visible signs of heart disease or arteriosclerosis. The respiratory and vascular systems were apparently in good shape. Yet there is absolutely no reason to believe his death was *not* natural. He had not ingested or inhaled any poisonous substance— and believe me, we checked that out *very* thoroughly. There were no signs in any vital organ of attack by any parasite, disease organism or virus—another thing we had to check carefully. Gilhart was apparently in excellent physical condition."

"What did he die of, then?" old Gilharrad sounded querulous, "Certainly not of a surplus of good health!"

Gilrae said patiently "As nearly as we can tell, he must have suffered a cerebral accident—in other words, a stroke, a blood vessel which burst deep inside his brain. Such a thing could easily elude even a careful autopsy, but having eliminated all other possibilities, that seems the only remaining one."

Natural causes. Gildoran knew he should feel relieved; but there was still a strange heaviness resting on his mind.

Maybe it's because it's my world—and it's turning sour so fast.

Gilban, the Chief Medical Officer—one of the few posts not rotated by lot every couple of years—stood up and said "I take it this means that we can again go down to the surface? I want to get the children down there as soon as possible. They need gravity experience."

"Yes, Poohbear spoke about that," Gilrae said. "We can go back down any time after we choose a new Captain." She looked, and sounded, inexpressibly weary. Doran wondered if she had eaten, or slept, since Gilhart's death. "And that's the next order of business—to choose a Captain. Who's on Nursery duty? Gilramie? Go down to Nursery, darling, and bring us up one of the babies for the choosing. And let's be thinking about Exemptions. You all know the rules. Year-Captains for the last seven years are automatically Exempt. Lori and Gilbarni haven't yet held three Class A positions; you're not qualified. Any Exemptions Requests?"

Gilban said shortly "I can't handle full Medic status and Captain too. Exemption?"

Gilrae looked around. "Any objections? All right, Ban, you're Exempt. Anyone else?"

Gilharrad said without rising "I'm too old, Rae. Can I be exempted too?"

"I wish you wouldn't ask," the woman said, "we need your experience, Harrad. Can't you take a one in fifty chance?"

"I didn't even *have* to come back to Active Status," the old man pointed out, and Gilrae sighed and said "Just the same——"

They were both distraught, Gildoran thought, or they would have remembered, and he tactfully broke the deadlock. "Gilharrad was Year-Captain less than seven years ago, Rae."

The woman shook her head, confusedly. "Of course he was. Anyone else?"

Gilrabin stood up and said "I'm going to have my hands full with Transmitter work. Exemption?"

"Any objections?"

"I object," said Gilmarti, a tall thin elderly woman, "There are eight of us in Transmitter, and we can manage if we have to. Raban can take his chance with the others."

"Exemption refused," said Gilrae, sighing. "Anyone else? All right, then, the rest of you put your identidisks into the box, and we'll draw as soon as Ramie brings up one of the children."

They rose and filed past the tumbling cylinder, each dropping his or her small metal disk inside. Raban was still grumbling. Gildoran paused beside Rae, wanting somehow to show his feelings, but she did not look up, and he sensed somehow that any stray word of kindness, a moment of sentiment, and the woman would break down. He put his disk into the box and found Gilmerritt at his side. She went back with him to the seat Ramie had vacated. She looked sad and strained. "Whoever the new Captain is, it's going to be hard, on us, and on him—or her. Everybody liked Gilhart. And if we get someone who actively doesn't *want* to be Captain, it's rough. I think anyone who asks should be Exempt."

"But most of us would rather stick with our own specialties," Doran reminded her. "There are only about eight of us on board who'd be willing to take the job and they're not always the best qualified. This is the best way, to make everyone take a turn sooner or later."

"I suppose so," she said, but she didn't sound convinced. Gildoran laughed. "Well, maybe you'll get it. Then you can build that resort you were talking about."

She shook her head and said seriously "Heaven help the ship if I'm Captain. I don't think I have any talent at all for leadership."

Gildoran thought, me too. This was only the second year he had been on the Qualified list. He looked around, and wondered how many of the *Gypsy Moth* crew were feeling just the same way.

Maybe we ought to Qualify people for Captaincy just as we do for Medic duty, or Nursery duty, or Engineering—talent, experience, interest, ability for leadership— if someone's tone deaf we don't make him lead music!

Gilramie came in, holding Gilmarina in her arms; everyone began to smile at the sight of the chubby child in her pink-and-white coveralls, her dark hair and rosy cheeks still marking her out from the others.

She's going to be dreadfully spoiled, she's everybody's

pet. The Poohbears kept the prettiest clothes for her, or is it just that they look prettier on her?

It crossed his mind suddenly, looking at Ramie's dark long almond eyes, that before she was bleached by space Ramie must have looked very much like Gilmarina. He couldn't remember back that far, but after all he and Ramie had been nurserymates, he *ought* to have some memory of a charming dark-haired pink-cheeked Ramie before she was six.

Ramie put Marina into Gilrae's arms, and the woman cuddled her close for a moment while Ramie dropped her identity disk into the tumbling box. Gilrae let it spin a moment; Ramie went to where she had been sitting, saw Gilmerritt there, and shrugged slightly, sliding into the nearest vacant place. Her look was neutral, but somehow Gildoran felt guilty.

Gilrae put out her hand and halted the spinning of the box. The small jangle of disks from the inside quietened slowly. She held Gilmarina down close to the box.

"Hand me one of the disks, Marina." The child plunged her chubby fist into the box. "Just one, that's right. Here, someone, take her . . ." with a small squeeze, Rae put Gilmarina into the arms of the nearest crewman. She turned over the disk and a strange look crossed her face.

If she's Captain it would be good for the ship but it might wreck her. No, she was Captain six years ago, she's exempt.

Gilrae, still with that strange expression, brought up the disk to her face and held it out.

"Gildoran," she said.

Gildoran blurted out, not believing, "Oh, no!"

She nodded slowly and came and put the disk into his hand. She added "Congratulations."

Gildoran was appalled at the irony of it.

His world. His responsibility.

And now his headache.

Gilrae touched his hand; clasped it within her own. She said "Don't look so stricken, Gildoran. Sooner or later it happens to everyone." But he fancied she was thinking that he was no substitute for Gilhart.

Suddenly the woman's face worked, as if she were going to cry, and Gildoran, acting on sheer impulse, reached out and caught her in his arms. He was so much taller that she hardly reached his shoulder, and she seemed helpless and vulnerable as he held her, trembling, against him. He felt that he would break himself with the strength of his own love, and yet . . . and yet to force awareness of himself, of his own problems and troubles, on Gilrae at this moment, would be the cruelest thing he could possibly do.

And then, with the first almost-pleasant thought he had had since Gilhart died, he realized that there was one thing he now *could* do; that was, in fact, his responsibility to do and no one else would do it if he did not.

He held his beloved gently, a little away from him, and looking down tenderly at her, gave his first command as Captain of *Gypsy Moth*.

"You're worn right out, Rae, and no wonder. It's time you got some rest. Gilban, take her down to the Infirmary, and give her a sedative. I want you to sleep the clock around, Rae. We're all going to need you, and we can't let you make yourself sick with overwork and strain."

She looked up at him in surprise and gratitude, and almost visibly, the strain in her face relaxed.

"All right . . . Captain," she said softly, and went with the Medic.

V

Four days later, and the clearing under the red cliffs was transformed. Four portable groundlabs dotted the area between cliffside and lakeside, and working from the landingcraft in flight, they had burned off an area of vegetation near the cliffs. This had meant the sacrifice of about half a mile of thick underbrush, mostly the thick bushes with the cup-shaped glimmering flowers, but it was that or the forest. Bushes were easier to burn, quicker to grow again if they had a stable place in the planet's ecology, and with the area cleared, there would be less chance of accidental fires near the camp when the *Gypsy Moth* set down.

Gildoran had established a temporary ground camp for the landing party plus the dozen-or-so experts who went out now, each day, making geodesic studies for the Transmitter Site. While theoretically it could be set down almost anywhere on dry land, there were a few practical considerations. It should not be on a serious fracture line or geological fault; Transmitters were better off without the possibility of earthquake damage, and so were the cities that inevitably grew up around them.

Everyone aboard had been—as the etiquette, and the tradition of *Gypsy Moth* demanded—ready to cooperate with the new Captain. Although Gildoran knew that at least half the crew was dismayed when he, the youngest of the qualified members, had been chosen by the relentless process of the lot, manners and long-standing decencies prevented anyone from letting Gildoran see it. Just the same, he had heard Gilnadir, from the Transmitter crew, say in disgust when he thought Gildoran out of earshot, "That boy—for Gilhart?" Gildoran had felt as embarrassed as if he had trespassed in hearing, rather than Gilnadir in saying, such a thing. He felt like yelling at Nadir "Don't you think *I* feel that way too? Do you think I *want* to fit into Gilhart's shoes?" Instead he had stealthily slipped out of the corridor, hoping Nadir wouldn't see him.

Just the same, he had not escaped an early confrontation.

The day after Gilhart had been ceremoniously committed to space for burial, Gilban of the Medic staff had approached him. Gildoran had asked "Is Gilrae all right?"

"She'll do. You did right to order her to rest, though, she was pretty near collapse. However, Captain, I'd like to know how soon you plan to go down again. We have to get the children downworld. They need to live in an iron-rich environment, they need sunlight, they need gravity. Can I order them down with the landingcraft today?"

He looked and sounded belligerent; a surly man, he was one of the few crew members taller than Gildoran, who had always been a little in awe of him. He had been Medic Chief since Doran's own childhood.

He temporized; "Have you talked to the Poohbears about it?"

Gilban brushed that aside. "I know how they feel about it, but they're not Medical experts. I think this is more important than someone's vague feelings." He pressed. "Can I order the Nursery camp set down today?"

There was no help for it. Gildoran said "I'd rather go along with the Poohbears feelings on the matter, at least for a couple of days, Gilban. They are, after all, the specialists on the well-being of the children." He fished for an acceptable excuse. "It might be more diplomatic not to antagonize them right away."

Gilban fixed the young Captain with a cold stare from long, yellow eyes; a stare which said more plainly than words that Gildoran could choose between antagonizing the Poohbears and antagonizing *him*. He said briefly "I've given you my opinion as Medical expert. Are you going to take it, or not?"

Gildoran said "Gilhart agreed to postpone it for further study and we are giving them land-based drinking water, which should remedy the iron problem right away. As for gravity and sunlight, according to the Poohbears, that isn't nearly so urgent. I think we should take a few more days on the planet to see what made Poohbear so uneasy about it."

Gilban said, teeth clenched, "Gildoran, you're the Captain, but I'd like to remind you that I was Chief Medical officer on this ship before you were out of the Nursery. Are you questioning my competence?"

This is bad. This is very bad. I'm going to need all the help I can get from the specialists, and I've already made Gilban furious. Does he think the power's gone to my head?

He said, desperately trying to placate the older man, "I would never question that, Gilban. But this isn't my own decision, it's Gilhart's. I don't want to question *his* competence, either. I don't feel free to set it aside until I have advice from everybody, including those who have actually been on the planet." He very carefully did not mention that Gilban hadn't.

Gilban said stiffly "Then I can't persuade you to trust my judgment."

Damn it, he was asking for it right between the eyes, and there was no way Gildoran could avoid it. "I'll always be ready to hear your advice, Gilban, after you've been down to the surface and made a study from there."

Gilban clenched his hands at his sides. His very tufts of hair seemed to bristle with wrath. He said "It's your decision to make, of course," and went away. And Gildoran knew that for the first time in his life, he had an enemy on the *Gypsy Moth*. Within hours of assuming his first command he had alienated one of the officials whose support would be most important to him.

Gildoran had posted no guards—extensive exploration in the landingcraft had shown no land animals of any sort, and no birds; in fact, no life form larger than the gleaming seven-inch butterflies who fluttered around the small dymaxion domes the crew had constructed for portable shelters. Ramie, walking at Gildoran's side across the burned area, smiled with pleasure at the iridescent shimmer of the creatures and said "I wonder if they're looking for the bushes we burned down? I hate to think of killing off such lovely creatures by destroying their food supplies."

"There are miles and miles of these bushes all along the range of hills," Gildoran said, "and if they're like most butterflies, these individuals would only live a few days anyway. A burnoff this size won't damage anything, and it will keep the insects away until we're sure if there are any deadly poisonous ones among them. Once we know, we can initiate control processes."

"These aren't poisonous, are they?"

Gildoran said "I'm no biologist, but Gilmerritt thinks not."

"What's the glitter on their wings? They look like jewels."

"According to our biological report, they almost are," Gildoran said. "A lot of life is based on hydrocarbons, and jewels are just crystallized carbon. Their wing surfaces are covered with, in essence, diamond dust—crystallized scales of microscopic carbon material. Diamond plated butterflies!"

Gilramie smiled. "I can see them becoming a fashion among some women. Remember how the glow-lizards on little gold chains became a fashion? Wear a live diamond-plated butterfly jewel. We should get a nice finder's fee for this world—it's beautiful!"

Gildoran smiled at the whimsy, and thought, again, how comfortable it was to be with her, when she could accept him simply as a companion. She must know by now that when he had moved into the Captain's quarters he had assigned the adjoining cabin to Gilmerritt and that they were together, but she had not spoken of it, and he was grateful.

He said "I take it you're down here as Nursery representative? I'm not keeping you from your work?"

"No, Gilban asked me to scout around and locate a good place for the children; drinking water, shade, reasonably away from the noise of the groundlab and equipment. I was tentatively thinking of the top of that little hill; the lake would be pleasant, but we're not sure yet about what forms of life the water might hold."

"Ramie, do you think I did wrong to refuse having the children down?"

"How do I know, Gildoran? I think you were wise to take the most careful course. Somebody's going to criticize you whatever you do," she reminded him, "Gilban thinks you're too careful, somebody else would grouse because you're too reckless. You're going to get the blame either way, so you may as well make whatever decision you think you can live with."

But she still looked troubled, and he asked "What's bothering you, Ramie?"

Her eyes sought out the edge of the clearing where the geodesic crew were running survey lines. "Gilharrad," she said slowly. "I think I would have forbidden him to come down to the surface. There's work enough for him aboard the *Gypsy Moth*. Are you sure he can handle the gravity?"

"He wanted to come, and Gilrae asked for him," Gildoran said. "That's the hard part of it, Ramie. I don't feel comfortable giving orders to people who were commanding the *Gypsy Moth* before I learned how to hold a slide rule—or for that matter, a spoon. For the children, I had Gilhart's decision to rest on."

"But you can't deny Gilrae anything," said Ramie shrewdly.

"Damn it, Ramie——"

"Oh, Doran—*don't!* I can't, either, how could I? But I'm worried about Gilharrad. Can't you send him up next time we break? He doesn't look right to me."

When they gathered for lunch in the clearing, Gildoran made a point of observing the old man, but although he was slow-moving and fragile, Gilharrad had good color. When Gildoran asked him, he declared testily that he'd never felt better, that the air was doing him good, and that unless this planet had his name on it, nothing down here could hurt him anyway. "You don't look too great yourself, young man," he finished, and Gildoran gave up. It was true, he had a headache. They all had headaches, and Gildoran suspected that if it wasn't the ozone, his at least was a purely psychosomatic headache; the result of having the weight, if not of the planet, at least of the *Gypsy Moth*, resting on his solitary shoulders.

I don't like this world. It's foolish, but I keep having this sense of impending disaster, and I don't like it.

Later that day Gilmerritt brought him a big sample box. "Did you ever see an insect who looked like a frog?" she asked, "Look at this fellow—an amphibious insect. But look at the big air-bladders in his chest!"

Gildoran looked at the huge red-striped creature. It did, indeed, resemble a monster frog, being almost eight inches long. "But it's really an insect?"

"No doubt about it."

The huge chest was puffed like a bellows. "He ought to have a monstrous croak," Gildoran commented.

"But that's the charming bit about it," Gilmerritt said, dimpling. "Listen. You don't hear a thing, do you?"

"No. But I've got such a headache I can't see straight, so I'm just as pleased he doesn't make a racket in proportion to his size."

"That's it," Gilmerritt said quietly. "That's why the Poohbear found this place noisy, and why Lori got sick, and why we all have headaches. The Poohbears evidently hear better than we do. Human ears only respond to sounds between, about, 16 cycles per second, and 20,000 cycles. This big fellow sends out subsonics—pulses at about nine per second. And everybody knows that subsonics will make people sick, give them headaches, feelings of fear and general malaise. We were reacting to soundless noise from the croakings of a giant frog."

Gildoran felt a sudden overwhelming relief. So that was the reason behind his vague unease, behind Lori's sudden sickness, behind the headaches and strange nameless fears. Pure, physical reaction to sound waves! "Can we get rid of the frogs in the area of the nursery camp?" he asked, and Gilmerritt nodded. "It will take a few days to round them all up, but I can bring down a subsonic detector to locate them. I ought to have thought of subsonics before—we have to damp them out for a mile or so around the Transmitter. So there's one of your problems on the way out, Doran." She touched the sleeve of his uniform, a curiously intimate gesture, and he smiled with relief.

"The subsonics won't do any physical damage?"

Gilmerritt shook her head. "Not unless they were of much, much greater volume than anything *this* size could give off. If this frogthing were the size of an elephant, now, he might be dangerous; as it is, he's just a pest. I thought you'd like to know."

Gildoran nodded, suggested she tell Gilban about it, and watched her go, thinking that, at least, one of their problems was ended. Once they knew that their malaise and headaches were due to a simple, physical and correctable cause, and once the frogbugs were rounded up and released out of earshot, the camp would become quite livable and this beautiful world could begin living up to its promise.

At that moment he became aware of a clamor of voices in the distance. At first they were only wordless cries, from the general area of the geodesic crew; then he realized that someone was calling his name. He began to run along the burned edge of the cliffs, apprehension surging up again almost to the panic point.

What now? What now, damn it?

It wasn't far enough to use the landingcraft, but too far for hearing.

Got to organize some surface transit down here.

Halfway he met them, a tight knot of crew men and women, clustered together, carrying something that was pale and terrifyingly limp, and with a hideous sense of replay, he knew that not *all* of his apprehension could be written off blithely to the subsonics.

Gilrae, looking even more white and shocked than at Gilhart's funeral, spoke the bad news in a daze.

"It's Gilharrad," she said, softly, "I saw him fall. There was nothing near him. He was tracing a fault line with the portable sonar gear. He didn't even cry out. He just clutched his hand at his head, and fell down. I wasn't three steps from him, and he was dead before I could reach his pulse. It was so sudden. So sudden!"

Over her bent head Gildoran met Ramie's dark accusing look. And Gildoran had no defense against those eyes.

"Call Gilban," he said wearily, "and have them take him up for an autopsy."

Poor old man, he wanted to die in space, he had earned it, I couldn't let him rest.

He asked the usual questions, hating what he knew it was doing to Gilrae. No, there had been nothing near him, nothing touching him. Was there anything about it that was like Gilhart's death? Only that it must have been very sudden, as he was passing below the cliffs. "Right there, behind that clump of bushes, next to the big grey-and-red striped rock under the clump of cupplants," young Gilbarni pointed out the spot.

Both deaths took place near the cup-plants. But that was ridiculous, Gilmerritt had tested every plant for organic poisons and in any case there was no trace of poisoning.

When he asked for an autopsy Gilban audibly snorted, but agreed, with the quite obvious attitude that he was humoring a power-mad dictator. That night, when they consigned Gilharrad's body to space for burial, Gilban gave him the results with weary patience.

"Immediate cause of death, obviously, a cerebral hemorrhage."

"Just like Gilhart?"

"No," said the big man testily, "*not* just like Gilhart. Gilhart was a vigorous man in the prime of life, and though he was subject to sudden cerebral accidents, like anyone else, it was evidently some sudden strain or attack. It could happen tomorrow to you or me. Gilharrad's real proximate cause of death was simply extreme old age. He was five hundred and seven years old, shiptime. In planetary time—God alone knows . . . centuries . . . Millennia—Several thousand years at least. He could have died of the same thing any time during the last thirty or forty years; the blood cells in his brain must have been as fragile as spiderwebs, and one of them simply gave way. You or I should live so long!"

Gildoran knew this was reasonable, but couldn't hold back a further question.

"Then you don't think there's any serious coincidence in the fact of two accidental deaths, from the same immediate cause, within a few days?"

Gilban looked disgusted. "I told you they were *not*, in effect, the same cause at all," he said. "You, or I, or one of the children of the Nursery, could die tomorrow of a cerebral hemorrhage, anyone could. Don't try to work up a big sinister tragedy out of nothing, Gildoran, just to justify your own fears about this planet. And by the way, I'm ordering the children down tomorrow. Gilmerritt assured me she'll have the subsonic frogbugs cleared out of that area by then."

Gildoran said "What do the Poohbears say?"

"I didn't ask them." Gilban's voice was cold. "I don't like having to remind you of this within a few days of your first command, Gildoran, but in emergency I have the authority to override even the Captain's orders on any strictly medical matter. I want those babies down in gravity and sunshine, Poohbears or no Poohbears—if they can't tolerate the noise, you can detail some crewmen for nursery duty. The babies won't hear the subsonics even if a stray frogbug gets into the camp. I'm not eager to throw my weight around, Gildoran, but the facts of the matter are, you've left me no choice."

Gildoran, having no choice himself, gave in as graciously as he could. That night in his quarters, he gave way to his secret doubts and miseries.

"What could I say, Merritt? I've no claim to be psychic. I think it's simply too much to believe, that they both died of the same thing, at nearly the same spot, within a few days of each other, but what can I prove? Am I supposed to wait for another death to convince him? Have you analyzed the cup-plants?"

"Only superficially," she said. "They seem to have some strange internal organs, I can't figure them out—I suspect they're for reproduction. I can tell you the cups have that glitter, because, like the frogbugs, they're covered with carbon crystals—tiny fragments of ruby, sapphire, diamond. There are other crystals inside and I suspect they "digest" live insects by grinding them up inside the cup-roots. I found a half-dissolved butterfly inside one of the internal organs, so that the cups operate something like a Venus flytrap. But there's no chemical poison involved—I doubt if anyone could eat one of the cups without one hideous tummy ache, but no poison, no gas—it was the first thing I checked." She hesitated and added "Anyway, the cup-plants are all burned off near the camp, just in case; shall I have them burn them off near the nursery too?"

It was a temptation. Gildoran had a definite dislike for the cup-plants, ever since he had seen Gilhart lying dead under a cluster of them. But he was a scientist, not a child. "No," he said slowly, "certainly not, if they're harmless. There's no sense in disturbing the ecology any more than we have to; we'll have to do enough clearing when we set down the *Gypsy Moth* andd get started on a Transmitter." He remembered that first thing tomorrow—in orbit around a planet, the *Gypsy Moth* observed day and night cycles—he would have to consult with Raban and Marti about a Transmitter location.

"I'd counted so on Gilharrad for advice," he said. "I forced him to come back. And it killed him."

Gilmerritt reached up and drew him down to her. She said softly, against his lips, "Hush, Doran. You know what he would have said to that: Planets and Space are all one Cosmos. And you know what he believed: for everyone, somewhere, there's a planet with your name on it. All we can do is the best we can, until the right one comes along. I won't tell you not to grieve, Doran. I loved him too. We all did. But there's nothing we can do for him, and we have to live."

Her mouth found his, gently, trying to give comfort and strength to his search. "All we can do is to live, Gildoran. And I'm here with you."

Why at this moment, drawing Merritt into his arms in a surge of sudden desire, did he think of Ramie's dark accusing eyes?

I ought to be with her, she and Gilharrad were so fond of each other, she felt the way Gilmarina would feel if I died . . .

He had enough problems aboard *Gypsy Moth.*
He wasn't going to add Ramie to them.

VI

"If the Test Transmitter works tomorrow, we can set the *Gypsy Moth* down and get started on the main Transmitter," Gilmarti said, and laid a group of printouts on Gildoran's improvised desk in the small dome. He handed them back to her without more than a glance.

"I'm not qualified on Transmitter, Marti," he said, "I'm leaving it to you and Raban." The old woman's face took on a quizzical look and he stiffened against it. Far too many of the crew, he knew, resented his youth. For the hundredth time he felt like reminding them that he didn't ask to be Captain. But they all knew that. Unexpectedly, Gilmarti smiled.

"Well, there's two kinds of knowledge," she said, "knowing what to do yourself, and knowing how to find someone else to do it for you. We're doing our part, Gildoran. We'll have the Test Transmitter ready in a few hours."

He followed her to the door of the dome and stood in the cloudy sunlight, looking across at the lake. He asked "Where are you going to set up?"

"Back against the cliffs. I've got a crew in there burning off underbrush to make walkways, and the Transmit receiver booth will be down by the lake. If the Test works out all right, we've got hardpan, with granite under it, and no fracture lines or faults as far as we can see. So we can set up the big one. Test Transmitters are intended for only a few ounces Transmission, of course —mouse-sized animals and small weights—so we can make the preliminary gravity and drift allowances. But once we have them calibrated properly, we can use the same calculations for the first big one to tie us in to Head Centre."

He saw that the old woman was still excited about it, said so, and she smiled at him. "It's always an exciting thing," she confessed. "Even after all these centuries. A new world tied into the Galaxy. And a chance to see what's been going on while we were tied in shiptime."

"How many years has it been?" Gildoran asked.

His friend on Lasselli's World—could he still be alive?

Marti frowned slightly. "I couldn't tell you without a computer tie-in and a slide-rule," she said, "but probably about ninety-seven years, downworld time. Does it matter?"

He shook his head. "Just thinking that the children in the hatchery where we got Marina and Taro and the others would be old people by now, and they're just out of diapers," he said. He saw that she was fidgeting, and remembered suddenly that, though she was four or five times his age it was up to him to dismiss her. "I'm sorry, Marti, I'm keeping you from your work. Let me know right away when you're set up and I'll come and see the test Transmission."

He stood for a moment in front of the dome, trying to organize his thoughts. He had initiated a practice of making the rounds of the camp every morning. One or two of the older officials acted as if he was trying to keep an interfering finger on their work, but most of the groups appreciated it. When Gildoran had been working, whether on the bridge, in the Medic labs or in the Nursery, he'd liked knowing that the Captain knew what they were doing and that they'd get a sight of him now and then to ask any necessary questions. The Poohbears always welcomed him to the Nursery camp; Gilrae was always glad to see him at the coordinating data dome, and Gilmerritt was always eager to show him what they were doing in the ecological studies. He had to walk warily with Gilban, but so far there had been no Medic emergencies except one of the Nursery six-year-olds who had skinned his knee in sliding down the rocks, a sore throat from a crewman who'd gotten wet collecting specimens from the lake, and a couple of sprained ankles and wrists from people unaccustomed to walking in gravity after all this time. The usual daily things.

Finally he decided that he would visit the biology groundlab first. In the ten days since Gilharrad's death they had learned some fascinating things about this world. Their first impression that there was no large animal life was correct—in fact, so far there was no warm-blooded life at all, only the complex interstructure of plant and insect. Gilmerritt spent much of her time in the field taking samples, but she admitted it would take years to work out the complexities of the symbioses and interdependencies between plants and insects. Her main work was to discover any dangerous plants or insects which should be avoided by the teams who would flood in from all over the Galaxy to finish opening up the planet.

She was in the field with her team when he stopped by the groundlab, so he went on. Gilrae was busy with weather charts, but greeted him with an affectionate grin.

"Doesn't it ever rain here, I wonder?" she asked.

"Is there any reason it should? I should think with this much overcast and cloud, there'd be plenty of water vapor in the air," Gildoran said but she pointed to a small furled electroscope and said "There's enough static electricity in the air that I'd expect some really monumental thunderstorms. Or else where's it coming from, and where does it go?"

"I'm sure you'll find out, sooner or later," he said, and she nodded. "Some day. Or else the teams coming in afterward will. I try never to get attached to a planet, Gildoran, or to care anything about it. Planets are for leaving."

I'm the Captain now, not a youngster, she can take me seriously. . . .

But he knew that she still shied away from emotion. Gilhart was too recently dead. He could love her, he could comfort her, but as for anything serious—no, it just wasn't in the records for now. Perhaps not for years, for years. . . .

Still, grasping at this moment of closeness and wanting to prolong it, he asked, "Do you still find it hard *not* to get attached to planets, Rae? From what you said to Gilharrad that day. . . ."

She said slowly, evidently trying to frame thoughts she had trouble putting into words, "Maybe it's natural for *homo sapiens*—to long for a particular horizon, a sky and sea of your own. Even Explorers were born in gravity, we're a downworld species, even if we try to be *homo cosmos*. We've built up our own taboos, but they're customs, not instincts. You know I'm a musician, I think that way. There's an old, old folksong, some of us used to believe it was pre-space, pre-Explorer. I'm sure you sang it in the Nursery, I know *I* did and I heard Ramie singing it to Gilrita and Gilmarina the other day." In her soft, husky voice, she hummed the melody;

"Far away you'll hear me call you
From somewhere across the sea,
Here am I, your special island,
Come to me, come to me.
Your own special home,
Your own special dream,
Far away in the sunlight,
How lovely they seem. . . ."

She broke off quickly. "They say there's a special island for everybody. A world you can't resist, a planet
with your name on it, that calls to you . . . that's why I
never could hate Giltallen when he found his, and left
us. . . ."

"I thought I'd found mine once," Gildoran said slowly.
His throat was tight with a surge of strange nostalgia, almost of homesickness, but for something he had never
known. "I thought it was my world, but it was only a
girl, and it was the wrong girl. But you've never found
yours, Rae?"

Her lips moved in a small smile. "Ah, that's a question
you should never ask, Gildoran. But I'll tell you this
much—this isn't the one that'll tempt *me* to stay. Not
nearly."

She bent briefly over her electroscope again and Gildoran said, with a start, "I ought to finish my rounds. I
get to talking to you, Rae, and the time just disappears."

She raised a slender hand to touch his cheek; almost a
gesture of love. He noticed for the first time in his life
that her beautiful hands were lined and seamed. She said
gently, "Rank still has its privileges, Doran. Relax. You
can stand and talk a few minutes without anyone having
the right to criticize you." Her smile turned impish. "But
Gilmerritt will scratch my eyes out if you spend *too*

much time making deep soulful conversation with me, so run along, Captain."

Gildoran laughed, slightly embarrassed, lifted a hand to her in farewell, and went on.

This isn't the world that'll tempt me to stay.
Me neither, Rae. I don't know why, but me neither.
Oh hell, there must be a frogbug around, I feel so damned apprehensive.

On the other hand, as he approached the Medic headquarters, he realized he didn't need a frogbug to feel wretched. Gilban didn't make a secret of his feelings, so he made his visit brief.

"Everything going all right?"

Gilban demanded briefly "Why not?" and Gildoran didn't press the point.

"Just making the rounds, Gilban. Let me know if you need anything or have anything to report. Carry on," and he took himself off again.

After that, I need a lift for my morale. How he hates me!

There was no sense in visiting the Transmitter site; Gilmarti had already reported and they'd send him word when the test was ready. He would like to see Raban, whom he liked, but there was no need for it. Gilnadir, in charge of the geodesic crew, quite obviously regarded him as too young for the Captain's job and just going through the motions. Gildoran suspected that Gilnadir thought it was part of his work to teach the Captain *his* job. He tended to overexplain, but he was polite about it. So he listened politely to Gilnadir talking about fracture lines to be avoided, sites of possible Earth slippage and rock slides, good building sites for cities, water supply.

"You realize, Captain, this planet hasn't a name yet. We've logged it by number, but it ought to have a name."

"Any suggestions?" Gildoran asked.

Come to think of it, I never found out who names planets. I guess I thought they came already named.

Gilnadir said, with careful patience, "It's the Captain's privilege to name the world discovered under his command. Gilhart hadn't gotten around to it. There's no hurry, though. Not until we register it with Head Centre."

"I see. I'll check the ship's library, then; I wouldn't want to duplicate anything we already have," he said.

Not that this is a world I especially want to bear my name. It's my world, but it's no prize.

"Make sure Rae gets copies of all these reports," Gildoran reminded him, realized a split second too late that this reminder was unnecessary and Nadir was a little offended by it. He amended the offense as best he could, and went off toward the Nursery.

It was the prettiest of the sites they had yet seen on this planet, located on a little hill a quarter of a mile or so beyond the lake, hopefully out of earshot of the frogbugs, and shaded by tall fronded trees with beautiful jewel-colored cones. The two domes—one for sleeping quarters, one for the Poohbears—were brilliantly colored, their triangular sections in brilliant primary colors. On the grassy slope in front of the domes, a group of six-year-olds were sitting on the grass having some kind of lesson in elementary mathematics, Ramie demonstrating with the sectioned rods and forms. They all scrambled to their feet to greet the Captain, then broke ranks and came to chatter questions at him. He spent a few minutes talking to the children, apologized to Ramie for breaking up her lesson, and asked where the Poohbears and the babies were.

"Gilrita and Gildando are napping," Ramie said, "I think Poohbear took Marina and Taro for a walk in the woods. They have more fun chasing butterflies. You should have seen Marina this morning, dressing herself up in the jeweled cones and trying to get a butterfly to stay on her shoulder for an ornament, the vain little monkey!"

"Did Gilmerritt give her okay on walking in the woods?" Gildoran asked, frowning. "We're not absolutely sure there are no poisonous plants or insects yet. This world could still have a few nasty surprises like the frogbugs."

"I thought I'd told you; Merritt's *with* them," Ramie said, "she was looking for leaf-samples. They only went off toward the edge of the forest."

"I think I'll walk that way," Gildoran said, feeling vaguely uneasy. Ramie gave him a faintly cynical look and said "I'm sure Merritt will be glad to have you—" then, relenting, "and I know Gilmarina will, she's been asking 'Why doesn't Doran come to see us, doesn't he love me any more?' "

Gildoran chuckled. "I've been missing her, too. When things settle down, I'll come down to the Nursery and give them some lessons." The six-year-olds began to clamor again to come with Gildoran, but he said severely "No, sit down all of you, with Ramie, and finish your lessons."

As he walked away he thought, damn it, now Ramie

will think I was making an excuse to be alone with Gilmerritt. Hell, we're *living* together, we don't need excuses, anyhow we'll have one of the Poohbears and two of the babies for chaperones!

The path they had taken was quite clearly marked, a natural separation between fronded bushes and low-growing flowers. He saw a pink ribbon lying on the path and picked it up, thinking that this was proof Marina had come that way, she loved pink and scattered her possessions broadcast. Well, he'd tie it back on her when he found them.

Several hundred feet into the wood, he began to hear voices, and turned in the direction of the sounds. Or was it the insects buzzing in their strange, high-pitched, droning tones? The woods were noisy, and he wondered how the Poohbears with their abnormally acute hearing —how far into the spectrum of sound did they hear?— could stand it. He felt like putting his own hands over his ears. There seemed an unusual amount of noise. . . .

Cosmos! Who was screaming? Gildoran began to run toward the sound, his heart pounding in sudden wild terror. A high-pitched shriek that sounded like Marina . . . a harsh, terrible howl like nothing he had ever heard before . . . screams . . . screams. . . . He crashed through the underbrush and his heart almost stopped.

A scene of disaster lay before him; Gilmerritt lay senseless on the ground. The great brown-furred Poohbear lay thrashing in agony, one of the babies clutched in her arms, a horrible howling moan coming from her lips. Beyond her a screaming, kicking rag of pink coveralls—*Gilmarina!* Gildoran heard himself shouting as he ran, snatching up the shrieking, writhing child in his arms. She kept on screaming in wild agony, and it was a minute or two before he could see that she was clutching at her small pink-sandalled foot. Then, with a final shriek, she went limp in his arms.

She was breathing, but the pink sandal was blackened and there was a great hole in it. Gildoran felt sick. He straightened, bellowing for help. Marina still cradled in his arms—he wanted to snatch her close, run madly with her for the Medic, but the others were part of his crew too, he couldn't leave them—he bent over the convulsed, moaning Poohbear. Her furry cheeks were contorted in agony, her loose lips drawn back to expose long yellow teeth. Only dimly could he make out what she was moaning. "My head . . . my head. . . ."

Ramie burst into the clearing, stared at them aghast. Gildoran shouted "Get the children inside the dome! Then get Gilban up here, and stretchers and a Medic crew—right away! Hurry!"

Ramie didn't even spend time asking questions or offering help. She ran. Gildoran gently detached the remaining child, Giltaro, from the Poohbear's arms. He was limp and lifeless. Gildoran could not tell whether or not he was breathing. He knelt beside Gilmerritt and saw that her eyelids were fluttering. She stared up at him with pain-glazed green eyes, moved her head faintly. "My hand. . . ." she whispered, "burn. . . ."

The whole hand was blackened like Gilmarina's sandal. She was obviously in shock, but there was nothing he could do for her. Gilmarina was breathing but unconscious, and Gildoran was glad she was spared the pain.

Giltaro was definitely not breathing now, and Gildoran could not find the faintest pulse in the little boy's chest. If they had been able to get a respirator or neurostimulator there within seconds. . . . The face had the same blue, twisted look he had seen that first day on Gilhart's face. *Cerebral accident.* Gildoran was aware that he was shaking with rage. Damn Gilban. Not even he could call *this* coincidence!

The Medic crew was there in minutes, and minutes later Gilmerritt and Poohbear were on stretchers and being carried down the hill; Gilban had pronounced Giltaro dead, and offered to take Gilmarina from Doran's arms, but he said "I can get her there as fast as you can," and strode down the hill to the Medic dome.

Gilban bent immediately over the Poohbear, while Gilnosta stripped off Marina's tiny sandal, looking in dismay at the blistered, blackened foot. "Cosmos," she breathed, "this looks like a laser burn! I haven't seen anything like it since the war on Martexi!" She dressed the hideous burn, gave her a spray-injection of painkiller, and turned to Gilmerritt.

"Will they live?" Gildoran asked.

"Gilmarina will make it," Nosta said. "Cosmos only knows how much good that foot will ever be to her, but she'll live. Merritt—she's in shock. If we can pull her out of it, she'll be able to tell us what happened within the hour." But she shook her head over the Poohbear, and Gilban looked grave.

"There's extensive brain damage. Even if she lives, she's likely to be a vegetable," he said. "I can't seem to stop the convulsions. She keeps going from one to the other. I'm afraid she'll never recover consciousness. What happened to them, Captain?"

It took a moment for Gildoran to realize that he was being addressed. "I don't know," he said, "I heard screams and found them all like that. I think Taro was already dead."

"But what was around them? Had they touched anything?"

Gildoran wanted to shout that he, Gilban, had been responsible for declaring the planet safe, that Gilban alone was responsible for Taro's death and the Poohbear's, for Gilmarina's crippling injury, Gilmerritt's terrible wound. But one look at Gilban's tortured face told him that there was no need to tell the Medic anything. In that moment, Gildoran knew the worst of command—in the last analysis, the Captain carries the burden of *everything*. It wouldn't help the dead and wounded to blame Gilban. He had honestly done the best he could. All he, Gildoran, could do now was to *help* Gilban, because they needed him.

He said, heavily, "I don't know, Gilban. Nobody knows. When Gilmerritt comes round perhaps she can tell you. Meanwhile, I'll send a biology team, *in space suits*, up there to explore, and find, if they can, what attacked them. There's evidently something there that no one knew about." With a last longing look at Gilmerritt he went to give the orders.

He did not hesitate an instant to order all the Nursery children up to the *Gypsy Moth* until the truth about this accident was known. The children were their future. They couldn't be risked. And now the *Gypsy Moth* was definitely short-handed, especially since someone would be needed to nurse the casualties night and day. His grief was deep and terrible for Giltaro. This was one of his own babies. He had jumped them across the Galaxy from the Hatchery. He had nursed them after the operations, had watched two of them die before they were even named. Now Taro was dead and little Gilmarina, her life spared, perhaps crippled for a lifetime. He ordered the Poohbears up with them. He had no doubt that whatever had killed Gilhart, and Gilharrad, had struck down the Poohbear too. She was probably dying. He wouldn't risk the others.

He was still waiting for the ordered spacesuits to be sent down—Transmitters from ship-to-ground *would* have been a help here—when Gilraban came to tell him the Test Transmitter was set up, and invite him to be present.

"Hold it off a while," he said heavily, "we can't set down until we know what hit them. We can't risk losing anyone else."

Raban grumbled, but he agreed. He also agreed to call in everyone from the woods and keep them inside the burned-over clearing area until they were certain what form of life had attacked the crew.

All that day a sort of stunned, sick silence hung over the clearing. Work was suspended, except for the biology crew in space suits exploring the clearing behind the Nursery where the accident had taken place. Gildoran wanted to put on a suit and go out there with them, to tear the place to bits and find out what had gone on there. But he couldn't even have that much satisfaction. He was the Captain. He belonged where people could find him and report to him.

He kept drifting to the Medic tent where Gilmerritt and Marina still lay drugged and the Poohbear twitched and muttered and moaned, then exploded, every few seconds, into another raging convulsion. Gilban looked haggard, his face almost grey.

"You can't stop the convulsions?" Gildoran raised his hand. "Not questioning your competence, Ban, only asking for information."

The man shook his head heavily. "We know so little about the Poohbears, even after all these centuries. They never get sick. They taught us most of what *we* know about medicine, but we don't know that much about *their* biology. When I give her enough sedative to quiet the convulsions, she goes into Cheyne-Stokes breathing —her heart stopped twice and I had to use a neurostimulator. All I can do is try the obvious support measures to keep her alive, and they're faililing anyway. It won't be long. A few hours at most; possibly a few minutes."

Gildoran said soberly "Should we get down the other Poohbears? Shouldn't they know she's dying?"

"What good would it do? They ought to stay with the children."

Gildoran said slowly "I think they have a right to say goodbye. Detail someone from the crew on the *Gypsy Moth* to look after the babies pro tem. And send up a shuttle for the Poohbears, unless you think it would be better to transfer her up in the landingcraft."

Gilban shook his head. "The minute we move her, she'll die. No question."

Gildoran went and stood over the great dying creature. Grief and rage tore at him. He looked down into the furry kindly face, distorted now and unrecognizable. A face like this had been the first he had seen emerging from the blur of his baby memories on the *Gypsy Moth*.

Our mothers. My mother is dying, and I can't do anything for her. Damn this world!

He looked at Gilban's bent shoulders, and thought with a pang that it was his mother too. On a deep impulse of pain, pity and the memories of a lifetime, he laid his arm around the older man's shoulders and for a moment they stood together.

He hates me. But we're brothers just now. We always will be. None of us have any world but this, or any people but each other.

He wanted to go on standing there, to weep like a child, to rage and demand of Cosmos why this had happened to them all. But he had work to do. He sighed heavily and went to do it.

The Poohbear who had been in the clearing died a couple of hours later. Gildoran was not present; he looked into the Medic tent and saw her great brown body surrounded by an impregnable circle of five other great brown furry backs, in a tight circle around the dying one, from which even Gilban was excluded. They were chanting softly in an unknown language.

Part of us for centuries. And we know nothing, nothing about them. They seemed as eternal as Cosmos, as deathless as the very stars.

Gilmarina had been sent up to the ship with the other children, under deep sedation. Gildoran went restlessly back to his own headquarters in one of the groundlabs, and Gilraban found him there.

"We can't do anything for the ones that are hurt, Captain. All right to go ahead with the Transmitter test?"

Gildoran had earlier told them to hold off, but now he shrugged. "Go ahead. Get it over with. One thing less to hold us up when we find out what the snag is. But be careful, Raban, we can't spare anyone else. What do you need?"

"Weights and some test animals. That's all right, we requisitioned them earlier, but the test animals we released on the surface are all behaving strangely."

Gildoran said absently, "Maybe we should have released test animals before coming down ourselves. Go ahead with your test Transmission, Raban."

Gilraban hesitated. "How is Merritt? Will she be all right?"

"I don't know. I'm going back to see. Gilban says she'll

live, but her hand is a mess, and she was still in shock when I was last there."

Raban said heavily "I'd go and see her, but I couldn't do anything—I'd only be in Gilban's way. Give her my love when she comes round, Doran."

"I will." When the thickset man had gone away, Gildoran walked aimlessly back toward the Medic dome. The cloudy sunlight was dimming under the perpetual haze, and it seemed to Gildoran that this day had been endless, and that he had spent all this long afternoon aimlessly shuttling back and forth between his own groundlab and the Medic quarters, not able to do anything in either place.

He wished Gilmerritt would regain consciousness, that she would open her green eyes and look at him and he could be sure he had not sent her, too, to her death on this world. He wished he could go up to *Gypsy Moth* and sit in the infirmary and cuddle Gilmarina in his arms as he had done when she was a tiny baby, trying to ease her pain and sickness with the warmth of his love. He wished he could call Gilrae from her work and keep her beside him and pour out all his own grief and misery into her sympathetic ears. He wished he could sit and mourn for little Taro, a part of the future they would never know. And he couldn't do any of these things. He was the Captain of the *Gypsy Moth*, and he was in charge of his own planet, which had turned out to be a world that bit back. All he could do was go on helplessly fighting against it.

VII

With a painful, repeated sense of *deja vu*—how many times today had he entered the Medic dome?—Gildoran shoved aside the hanging panel and stepped inside. Then he recoiled, for a great darkness blocked off the light and kept him from entering. With a split-second of shock, almost of fear, he saw that the five living Poohbears were massed before him, looming over him; barring his entry to the Medic dome.

"May I come in, please?"

"No," said one of them, "you may not. *E-te-ragh-o-mana*, our sister is gone, she has left us on this world of hell and darkness, and we are lost, we are alone and desolate."

He looked up into the inscrutable animal faces. He was abruptly, shockingly conscious that after all these years he was among strangers, he had always called each of them, interchangeably, Poohbear. Now for the first time he heard the strange alien name she had borne, and he wondered if they were among the peoples who allowed their true names to be known only after death.

None of them had died in living memory.

He said helplessly, trying to placate, "Poohbear, all of you, we too have lost our brothers. Gilhart has left us leaderless. Gilharrad and all his wisdom have gone into

124

Cosmos, Giltaro lies dead with all the promise of his youth never to be known. We share your grief, you know that we all grieve with you, but we are all together in misfortune."

The unreadable brown faces held no visible emotion, but it seemed to Gildoran that there was both fury and contempt in the soft voice that answered him.

"You people are of short life and shorter memory. Every few years you take to yourself children of your people and you can bear to see half of them die like flowers never opened. Every little turn of the century you know you will lose your brothers and sisters. To you death is only a moment, some one else is taken into the place of the dead and it is as if he or she had never lived. I have seen a hundred of you come and go, die and be forgotten. Do not presume to compare your grief with ours, which is unending and eternal. We have lost a part of ourselves and we shall never again be as we were before."

Before the words, like a strange compelling dirge, Gildoran bent his head. What could he say?

Man that is born of woman is of few days and born to sorrow. . . .

How indeed, could he guess at their grief? Was this why the Explorers were hated by the downworld mankind, because they seemed, in human memory, almost undying? Did the downworlders believe they were immune from grief because no downworlder saw them age and die?

But he lifted his head and faced the Poohbears steadily.

"Grief is not less because we must meet it more often and we must learn to live every day of our lives with it," he said quietly. "In your sorrow perhaps you do not know this, Poohbear. Grieve as you must. As we all must grieve. Perhaps in your grieving you will learn to know us better, and we you. What now can we do for you? Will you have us bury her here? Or shall we consign her to Cosmos as we do our own?"

Silence for a long moment, and the looming Poohbears seemed to close round him. And Gildoran thought, they were about to kill him then, but they opened a path for him. A third said, still in that cold contemptuous furious tone, "Our lost one told your people that we should not be here, nor your children. The loss of your little ones is the price you have paid for your foolishness in refusing to hear our wisdom. We shall care for her as it is fitting that we do. Let us carry her forth."

Gildoran said flatly, "None of you are going anywhere on this planet, unless you all want to follow her and die. I'm sorry. I'll make what concessions I can to your rites for the dead, but I can't let you go out there where you can all be killed. I can clear one of the domes or ground-labs and let you have it to yourselves. Or I can arrange to send you all up to the *Gypsy Moth*. Whatever you say. But no one from *Gypsy Moth* goes out of sight on this world until we know just why the deaths happened and what we can do to keep any more of them from happening."

Again their huge forms seemed to close in around him, dwarfing him, looming over him, and Gildoran felt engulfed, terrified. Then the great furred bodies drew back, opening a way for him, and one of them said "Be it as you will, but we must be alone. We will go up to the ship and there we will learn to live with our unending grief."

As one they turned their backs on him and, taking up the body of their dead, carried her out of the dome. Gildoran got in touch with Communications from the nearest groundlab for a landingcraft to take them up, and while he was at it, detailed four or five of the skeleton crew still aboard *Gypsy Moth* to take over in the Nursery. Somehow he knew, knew for a fact and without being told, that the Nursery would see nothing of the Poohbears for a long, long time.

When he finally put the communicator aside, he leaned his aching head in his hands. What next? He raised his head to see Gilmarti standing before him. He said wearily "What now?"

"First test Transmission results," she said formally.

He shrugged. "Not now. I suppose it went off about as usual, didn't it?"

"No," she said grimly. "Oh, it operated. But the final results were all out of whack. The weights lost a few micrograms. And the test animals all died."

Gildoran pressed his fingers to his aching head. Of course. Murphy's Law, the law older than space—anything that can possibly go wrong will go wrong.

A Transmitter failure. He had never known a Transmitter setup to fail. He had used them, without thinking, since he was old enough to walk, whenever he was on a planet tied into the world-net. He knew that if one failed, his atoms would be scattered all over the Cosmos, but they never failed. But then, Poohbears never died, either. Nothing was the way it should be on this world and he might as well stop expecting it.

"Do you have any idea why, Gilmarti?"

"Probably our instruments aren't working right. We need to check out the magnetic field of the planet again —double-check it. It's not radiation, we studied that; enough radiation to throw off a Transmitter would have us all dead already. After all, they operate in full Cosmic-ray fields."

But Gildoran was thinking of the singed fur of the Poohbear, the burnt and blackened sandal on Gilmarina's tiny foot, Gilmerritt's ruined hand. Radiation burns? He spoke to Gilmarti about this, but she shook her head.

"Radiation burns don't look or act like that," she said. "I haven't time to educate you about them now, Gildoran, you learned that in Nursery."

"You're right, of course. But if not radiation, what? In Cosmos' name, what *is* it on this planet, Gilmarti?"

The woman said grimly "You tell me and then we'll both know. You're the Captain; that's *your* job. Mine is to get a Transmitter functioning. Yours is to fix things so I can do mine."

She's right, of course. Yet what can I do? I can't say it's somebody else's fault. Ultimately everything that happens on the *Gypsy Moth*—or any world we're on—comes back to me. No wonder we change Captains every year! Who could live with this job any longer than that? No wonder people struggle to get Exemptions.

He said "Well, all I can do, Gilmarti, is to give you a clear field to requisition any equipment you need to check it out. But not tonight. You look dead. Get some rest, and start again tomorrow. Raban, too. The Transmitter can wait."

"Right, Captain," she said, "although as short-handed as we are, the sooner we tie into the world-net again so we can pick up some more children and supplies, the better."

She was about to leave, but he motioned her back for a minute. He said "Gilmarti. Just hypothetically, what if we had to abandon this world—not tie it in at all? Suppose we never get a Transmitter working at all here? What then?"

She thought that over. "It has happened, of course,"

she said. "Usually we find out that a world isn't suitable before we set down on it. We'd need more fuel, of course, for the converters, before we leave. Anything will do, of course—rock if there's nothing else. Anything that breaks down into hydrogen atoms, under fusion. But if we're too short-handed to set up a Transmitter we could be too shorthanded to work ship."

He didn't tell her the Poohbears were, for all practical purposes, on strike and some of their precious personnel must be used in caring for the children. He said "Well, keep it in mind, Marti, it could happen. Get what equipment you need to check out the trouble with the Transmitter."

"It would be easier if we could set *Gypsy Moth* downworld, instead of trying to dismantle the equipment and bring it down in the landingcrafts."

He nodded. "I know, but we can't do that yet. As long as some of us are up there, we can't *all* meet with freak accidents. Do the best you can, Marti. Make a computer tiein if you need to. But I can't order *Gypsy Moth* down till I'm sure. Maybe not at all."

She seemed to see that he'd said his last word on the subject and turned to go. Abruptly she looked back.

"Captain," she said, "Gildoran, have you eaten anything today?"

He realized he hadn't. It was no wonder he felt woozy.

"I've no right to remind you of this," Gilmarti said, "it's not my job. But part of yours is to keep yourself fit to do it."

"I haven't felt like taking the time——"

She said quietly, "If you don't it's everybody's business. If you'll forgive me for making a suggestion——"

"Please do." I need all the help I can get, he thought, but he didn't say so. Part of the help *they* needed was something he couldn't give them; confidence in their Captain. Somehow he *had* to give it to them.

"Short-handed or not, detail somebody to wait on you and arrange to look after your routine needs," Gilmarti said. "No Explorer is servant to another—I know that. But your time belongs to the crew, and you have no right to spend it looking after things like hunting up your own meals and sorting your uniforms. It's not a question of privilege. I know you'd hate that as much as any of us would. But when you take time for that sort of thing, you're neglecting your own work—and stealing time from us. Get someone like Lori or Gilbarni, whose work can be duplicated, and detail them for it."

She went away, having said her piece, and Gildoran got on the communicator again and asked for Rae, who had personnel records at her fingertips, to send him someone with something to eat.

He was learning more about command all the time. Maybe that was why they never gave you any special training for the job. You learned it through experience—fast—or you didn't live through it.

When he had eaten and snatched a brief nap, he went back—he'd lost count by now—to the Medic dome. The body of the Poohbear was gone. Gilban was asleep, dead exhausted, on a folding-cot; Giltaro's body was gone. Only Gilnosta, looking white and weary, sat beside the sleeping Gilmerritt. It was completely dark outside now, and a dim light fell on the woman's face.

"How is she, Nosta? Has she recovered consciousness?"

"Not really, but I'm expecting her to come round any minute. I imagined you'd want to see her." For a moment Gildoran was thinking that Nosta was speaking of the relationship between them, but the young Medic added, "You'll have to ask her what she knows about the accident, she's the only one who may be able to tell you anything."

So he wasn't even allowed to express normal concern, anxiety about his paired-mate; just information about an accident to crewmembers! He went and stood beside the unconscious woman. A few days ago she had been just another crewmember and everyone on the crew had been expecting him to settle down with Ramie. Then Gilmerritt had suddenly emerged from the crew as part of his close-in world, had come sharply into focus for him, had moved into the center of his life. He looked down at her with a curious mixture of tenderness and concern.

This woman is my mate, my partner, we've committed ourselves to share our lives, our bodies, our loves, and yet . . . and yet. . . .

Just now, all she could really be to him was the key to the mystery of what was killing his crewmen. He pressed his hands to his head, wishing somehow he could clarify his confused thoughts.

The ship in confusion and chaos, and I'm worrying about my own personal love life?

Against the pillow Gilmerritt stirred and he leaned forward and clasped her unbandaged hand. She opened her green eyes, dark with pain.

"Gildoran?" she whispered, and he saw her look slowly around the Medic dome, trying to orient herself in space and time.

"I'm here, Merritt. How are you feeling now?"

131

He saw pain move across her face. "My hand. It hurts. It hurts terribly. The children—how are the children? I heard Gilmarina scream——"

"Gilmarina's foot is in the same shape as your hand. Giltaro must have died instantly," he said, and saw her face crumple in anguish. "Poohbear died this evening."

Her free hand clutched convulsively at his, but she did not sob.

"Merritt. Darling, can you tell us what happened?"

Slowly she shook her head. "I'm not sure," she said, and he saw her features twitch again as if in memory. "The children were picking flowers, and one of the flowers . . . burned them? Burned me? There was a sort of light—no, I didn't see anything. But the plant . . . it screamed. It screamed like Gilmarina, and it whipped at me. And then . . . I don't remember anything more, except that Poohbear fell across me, and I smelled something like burning meat." She frowned and added, confusedly, "It must have been my hand burning, and then I thought I heard you a time or two, and then . . . I don't remember any more."

Her eyes slipped shut again.

The plant—it screamed?

So the plants were the danger. Gildoran realized that without being aware of it, he had suspected it all along. Gilhart had died in a group of cup-plants. Gilharrad, too. Had the portable sonar gear somehow frightened them? But plants that could emit burning rays? How? Damn it, *how?*

Gilmerritt's eyes flickered open again.

"Will I have the use of my hand?"

Gildoran looked at Gilnosta. The Medic said honestly "It's too soon to tell. When we can spare you for a year, to get you into a suspended-animation tank and grow you a new one, yes, of course. But until then—no, Merritt. I don't think so. And we're too short-handed—excuse me, dear—to give you a year off."

The woman's eyes squeezed shut. The fingers of her good hand clutched spasmodically on Gildoran's, but she made no protest. There was nothing he could say. In the shape they were in, Gilmerritt could not be spared. Hands or no, they needed her mind, her intelligence, her directing force in the biology labs. Gildoran faced, grimly, the knowledge that it might be a long time before they could spare Gilmerritt for the year she needed in suspended animation to grow a new hand replacing the one which had been virtually burnt off. With one of the children dead and another crippled—although Gilmarina could go at once into a regrowth tank, as soon as there was someone to tend the tank—it would be years and years before they could spare a single crewmember, even a one-handed one. They couldn't spare Gilharrad, he had come back to them, and now even his frail help was gone.

Gilmerritt drew her hand away from his, turned her face away and lay in a stubborn, withdrawn isolation. And Gildoran understood that, too. Now he must bear the weight of Merritt's disability as well as everything else. All at once he felt broken, overwhelmed. All day, without knowing it, he had been waiting for Merritt to recover, to regain the lost part of himself. Burdened, overwhelmed with his own losses and griefs, he had still hoped somehow that among so much loss, at least Merritt's love for him would be unchanged, that he could rest for a little while in the certainty that had been theirs as a couple. Now that was gone, too.

Then Gildoran was appalled at his own selfishness. Had he been expecting Merritt, in her pain and loss, to

133

comfort him for *his?* All he could do for her now was to love her, and to accept even her anger and withdrawal. Disregarding her turned-away face, he kept hold of her good hand until she relaxed and slipped back into sleep. Perhaps what had been between them had not been deep enough to survive this shock. But it had not been merely a surface adventure either, and he would stand by her and do what he could for her, even if she turned away from him.

This damnable planet! This hellish world! It seemed that ever since they first touched down on it he had been going from one crisis to another, without an instant's pause!

Gildoran's world! Cosmos, what a wretched, ironic joke *that* was!

VIII

Gildoran had slept for a while in his groundlab before the crew working in spacesuits came in with their reports. They had checked the clearing and the plants, one by one, and had been able to find no trace of poisonous plants, plants which moved on attack or plants which secreted chemicals capable of causing such burns as the ones which Gilmerritt and Gilmarina had suffered. "We can analyze the plants section by section and organ by organ," Gildorric offered, "but Gilmerritt did that already."

"Then are you trying to tell me the accidents never happened?"

"No," said Gildorric, "but we still don't know *how* they happened, or what the mechanism is." He smiled, grimly, his bare head sticking out of the spacesuit. "Maybe the plants were on their good behavior. No headaches, even." He added, "Maybe it's just that the helmets screen out sounds too. I couldn't hear those damned frogbugs either."

"Sound. . . ." Gildoran broke off. The Poohbears had abnormally acute hearing. Human hearing went from 16 cycles a second to about 20,000. The frogbugs put out sound at about nine cycles, subsonics. But there were other sounds which humans couldn't hear. A whole spectrum of them, up above 20,000 cycles. And if the frog-

135

bugs were giving off subsonics, maybe other insects, or even plants, were giving off other sounds.

"I can't disturb Gilmerritt again," he said, "who else is here from the bio groundlab?"

"I know my way around in there," young Gilbarni said.

"You brought down test animals and released them. Are there any bats among them?"

"*Bats?*" Gilbarni stared at him as if he had gone mad. "I think there are some bats in the hibernation sector, in the ecology-niche equipment. If you really want one, sir, I can send up to *Gypsy Moth* and tell Gilmarlo to thaw a few out and send them down. You mean *bats*, sir? The things that fly——"

"And see in the dark, and find their way around by emitting ultrasonic radar shrieks," Gildoran confirmed. "Yes; send for some. And get down some oscilloscopes and a standard-scale vibration measuring device with extra short-pulse equipment on it. Meanwhile, everybody get some food, it's going to be a busy day."

Gilraban said "We have the equipment to check the Transmitter, Captain. Shall we go ahead?"

Gildoran shook his head. "Nobody outside the clearing except in spacesuits," he said, "until we check out my theory. Nobody near *any* plant that grows on this world, or any insect either."

Gildorric was frowning, trying to follow what he was saying. "You're thinking about ultrasonics? But . . . Marina and Merritt were *burned*, Doran. Gilhart and Harrad died of cerebral hemorrhage, and so did Giltaro. Are you trying to tell me——"

"I'm not telling you anything, yet," Gildoran said, "let's check it out first. But I should have guessed, when I heard that Gilharrad had been using the portable sonar-gear—that sends out pulses of ultrasonics which bounce off solid layers of rock. My guess right now is that he scared something, and it struck back. If I'm right, it could explain everything. We'll know, now, in a few hours."

It was dusk again when, spacesuited, they walked toward the clearing behind the now-deserted Nursery camp. Other workers in spacesuits were taking down the brightly-colored structures and only the skeleton-like dome framework remained, green bushes and trees clearly visible through the empty triangular segments. The spacesuit helmets closed out all sounds, even the eerie squeaks of the bats in their cages. Inside the clearing Gildoran stopped and gestured to the others to release the creatures. One by one they fluttered up into the dark sky and began to circle there, and Gildoran visualized them sending out their high, ultrasonic pulses of sound—

And then, one by one, their fluttering ceased, turned into aimless confused flight. One by one they fell, like small stones, into the clearing at the Explorers' feet; some feebly moving, others already dead. Gildorric, bent over an oscilloscope, nodded grimly.

"I thought so. The minute they started sending out their pulses of sound, the sound waves started coming from all over—zapped them, one by one. Evidently the plants here—mostly the cup-plants, but others too—and some of the insects, send out sound waves between 30,000 and 100,000 cycles per second. Most of them are fairly weak, but those diamond-like crystals in the cup-plants, and probably a few others, act as piezoelectric crystals in ordinary electric equipment."

Gilraban said "Then that's what fouled up the Transmitter test."

"Right. Too much stray energy around which we didn't know about and hadn't compensated for," Gilmarti said. "Then that explains the deaths——"

"Right. And the brain damage. And the burns. Sound

waves at various frequences can kill—and these must have been pretty narrowly focused—or can burn as badly as a laser," Gildoran confirmed.

Gilraban said in deep disgust and despair "Why did none of us think of it?"

Gildoran said heavily "Because we weren't looking for it. I suspect it's a unique evolution on this planet—ultrasound is usually associated only with technology. At least that settles it finally. No one to go out without spacesuits again, except in the burned-over areas where there's no plant life left. Get what fuel we need, right away. We'll have to decide what to do."

But he knew, as he took the shuttle up to *Gypsy Moth* that evening, that the "we" who would decide would be ultimately himself. Gildoran. That was what it meant to be Captain.

He had called together the most experienced officers on the *Gypsy Moth;* Gilrae, Gilban, Gilraban for the Transmitter crew, half a dozen of the older ones. He thought, with deep bitterness, of Gilhart and Gilharrad. They were so badly needed. And Gilmeritt, lying drugged and crippled in the infirmary; and of Gilnosta, who had been relieved of all her other duties to nurse her and Gilmarina until they were out of danger.

"The crux of the matter is," he said, after briefing, "that we are desperately short-handed. We were shorthanded before; now we could almost say that *Gypsy Moth* is crippled. Is there any way to salvage this world? I admit frankly that I don't know; I haven't the experience. Raban, could we set up a Transmitter and get through to Head Centre? With a complete Terraforming team, we could probably transform this world into a fairly safe one."

Gilraban said "I don't know. I don't think so. It would take months to compensate for the ultrasonics all over the planet, unless we wanted to make a major burn of plant life—virtually strip it bare. Meanwhile we'd have to live aboard *Gypsy Moth* and commute down from groundlabs—we couldn't make a setdown. And work in spacesuits. Besides if we stripped the planet . . ." he shrugged. "What would they want a Transmitter here *for*, then?"

Gildoran had been afraid of that, but he put the next question anyway. "Gilmerritt could answer this better, but . . . Marlo, can we possibly kill off enough of the *lethal* plants to work here?"

Gilmarlo, the second biologist, said, "Not without a major ecological study; probably not then. Put it this way; if you kill off the most dangerous plants, their natural enemies—the most lethal insects—thrive, and you'll have an insect plague. After that, the insects overpopulate, and kill off even the harmless plants. Then you've got bare rock. Even if we all worked triple shifts it would take nine or ten years shiptime to replace everything with a stable ecological cycle of harmless plants and animals. No, Gildoran. I'm afraid I agree with Raban. We've got to write this one off. We don't have the personnel, we don't have the biologicals, we don't have the *time*. And," she added with a sort of bitterness, "we don't have Gilmerritt."

Gilban said harshly "Don't blame the Captain, Marlo. I overrode him. Don't you think I know it's my fault that we've lost so many——"

"No, Ban, that doesn't get us anywhere," Gildoran interrupted. "We could blame ourselves and each other all day and all night, if we wanted to. If I'd been sure of my facts instead of relying on instinct; if any of us had been willing to question the Poohbears and find out what it

139

was they didn't trust. . . . You did the best you could on the available information; leave it at that. Your job now is to get the hurt ones back in shape."

He turned to Gilrae. If anyone could manage to pull any kind of victory out of what looked like total defeat, she would be the one. "Rae. You've had a lot of experience with planets that looked hopeless. With Harrad and Hart gone, you're almost our senior working Officer. Can you see any way out, short of simply abandoning this planet?"

Gilban muttered "I don't see why we should even think about it."

Rae looked first at the Medical officer and said "I know what Doran's thinking, Ban, and he's absolutely right. We've poured too much into this planet to leave it without trying to recover at least *some* of our losses. We're desperately short-handed; we're crippled. With the Poohbears on strike, we're *worse* than crippled. It's going to be hard to work the ship; it's going to be even harder to hold out until we find another usable world, or until the children grow up. If we could think of a way to save something out of this disaster, we ought to." But she had said *if we could* instead of *if we can,* and Gildoran knew it was hopeless, even as she went on "But I'm still remembering what Gilhart said just before we landed— 'Now and then you meet a world that bites back, and all you can do is run'—while you still have something to run with. If we hang on here, we'll run the risk of further losses, and there isn't any real hope of gains to make up for them. I agree with Raban, Gildoran. We'll have to let it go."

Gildoran nodded, slowly. She was right. There wasn't the slightest chance of anything salvaging the disaster of his first command. He might as well go and make it official.

As he went slowly down the shaft toward the bridge, Rae followed him; touched his shoulder lightly.

"Gildoran——"

"I really made a mess of it, didn't I, Rae? My first planet, and my first command——"

He had halfway expected comfort, but she frowned at him. "That is sheer self-indulgence, and you know it," she said. "Don't flatter yourself by thinking that you *could* have thought of a way out. There simply wasn't any. Sometimes there *isn't* any happy ending, Gildoran. It's human nature to want one. If it's any comfort to you, I don't think Gilhart could have handled it any better. But we'll never know. We've done the only thing we could; now all we can do is try to put it behind us and go on to the next thing. If you want a shoulder to cry on, try Ramie!"

It was like a bath of ice-water. He felt the surge of adrenalin like a metal taste in his mouth; too angry to speak, he jerked on his heel and turned away toward the bridge.

Behind him he did not see that Gilrae's face softened and there were tears in her eyes. He strode angrily into the bridge deck without thinking, moved into the spot where he had seen Gilhart sitting last.

Slowly, he pulled the ship-to-ground communicator toward him. Lori, at the scanner, looked up expectantly, but he paid no attention to the child.

"All hands, ship and groundlabs, this is the Captain," he said heavily. He knew that his voice was going all over *Gypsy Moth*, a rare thing, and only for official statements such as this. "By joint decision it has been decided to abandon the planet. Geodesic crew, abandon all exploration efforts and detail crew working in spacesuits to load fuel and metals for ship reserve and raw material for the converter. Dismantle all groundlabs, dismantle test Transmitter and return to *Gypsy Moth,* suspending all operations. We will depart the planet one shiptime day from this moment."

Now it was official. He had given the orders which would make permanent the fiasco of his first command. He replaced the communicator slowly and looked into the big screen. It was a beautiful planet lying below them, wrapped in its veils of blue-green, gleaming faintly like an iridescent jewel in its own sun; but it was as deadly as poison.

He thought of Gilmerritt, who had wanted to build a beautiful resort world there; of Marina with the jewelled butterfly on her shoulder. Leaving the planet behind would not solve their problems. We'll have to spare Gilmerritt some time soon, get her into a tank for a new hand, he thought. But when? With the Poohbears on strike—and three deaths—we'll need everybody. The problems had only begun, and this was only the beginning of his year of command. There were two gravely wounded crewmembers to be healed. There was Gilban's self-confidence to be restored. He would have to persuade some of the older Floaters to come back to modified duty. The Poohbears must be coaxed back somehow. Ramie was working single-handed in the Nursery. . . . He looked down at the great blue-green planet below.

You didn't get us, after all. You're just another planet, and you're for leaving, like all the rest.

"Captain . . ." Lori said timidly. He sighed, wrenched his gaze from the bewitching ball of blue-green cloud beneath them and said, "What is it, Gillori?"

"How shall I log this? The planet has no name in records, and it should be transmitted to Head Centre when we can."

With a shock Gildoran remembered that it was his privilege to name the planet.

Gilhart, he thought. A permanent memorial to the world which had, after all—in the phrase of the Explorers—had his name on it.

Revulsion struck him. He could just imagine Gilrae's accusing eyes if he gave her lover's name to this hellish world. Better to take the blame himself. Gildoran's world? Cosmos, no!

"Log it as Hellworld," he said, and thrust his seat aside to take a last look at the planet below. "I'm going down to Nursery, to see how Marina is getting on, and what the Poohbears are up to."

Others could handle the details of getting the crew and the groundlabs pulled in, loading fuel and raw material for converters and reserves, navigating away from the planet.

His world now was the *Gypsy Moth,* and every soul aboard her was his personal responsibility. Ramie, trying to handle eight children, one seriously injured, would have to be given help, and he should ask her what she needed and wanted. She wouldn't have any questions except the necessary ones, and she would understand that he had done the best he could, as she always understood. Gilrae's taunting phrase, 'if you want a shoulder to cry on, try Ramie's,' came back to him, he thought he might just do that, sometime.

He said formally "Lori, the bridge is yours," and turned his back on the scene of his first command.

Part Three

A WORLD WITH YOUR NAME ON IT

". . . you'll hear me call you
From somewhere across the sea,
Here am I, your special island,
Come to me, come to me.
Your own special home,
Your own special dream. . . ."

I

"Nobody's talking about *blame*," Gilrae said wearily.
"It's bad luck, that's all. Two impossible planets in a row.
What I'm talking about is *facts*, Gilban. The fact that
we're crippled. The fact that we now have no functioning biological officer, with Marlo killed on Tempest, and
Merritt only able to direct. The fact that we have literally too few hands to work ship, even with Rita and Gilmarina and the other children working two hours a day
on messenger service and such instead of doing lessons."

Gildorric smiled without mirth and said "I once said it doesn't happen twice in a lifetime. Now it's happened twice in seven years. If it happens again, we're dead."

Gildoran looked around the Ship's Council. He was attending now as a senior officer, since the death of Gilraban in the disaster on Tempest. He said "We were already short-handed after Hellworld. It was bad then, with the Poohbears on strike, and all of us, after we worked full shiptime shifts, taking an extra hour every day to tend Gilmarina's regrowth tank."

"Which means at least we have Gilmarina able to function now," Merritt said, with a clinical glance at her own crippled hand.

Cosmos, we've got to fix it somehow so we can give Merritt a year free, or she'll be our next casualty.

Gilban followed his glance. "So I was wrong again," he said bitterly, "believe me, Merritt, I had hoped——"

"Oh, don't," she said harshly, "I've heard it all before. You didn't know Marlo would be killed on Tempest. There's no point in I-told-you-sos. You gambled and lost, but it was me you gambled with. Am I supposed to be happy about it?"

Gilrae said "This is all beside the point. Blaming Gilban is foolish. Let me remind you that if he hadn't devised a way to get rid of the contamination from Tempest, we'd have lost more than a landing-party—we'd *all* be dead with the cold-death."

Gilmerritt did not answer, and Gildoran guessed she was thinking that it would have been better that way. He reached out and encircled her wrist gently with his arm.

He found himself wondering briefly whether it was loyalty or love which had kept him bound to her, standing between her and her own desperate moods of bitterness and despair, her near-suicidal whims, for six years now. Did it matter? Somehow she needed him, and he could not desert her.

He wondered if he still felt guilt, or responsibility, for the Hellworld disaster that had lost her the use of her hand. No matter; he had been *there*. And no one else felt able to take the responsibility for Merritt's will to live. But it couldn't go on much longer.

He should have taken a stand, that first year when he was Captain and had had the authority. He could have faced down Gilban, insisted that it was no harder to tend two regrowth tanks than one. Then after the Tempest disaster, which had lost them a fourteen-man landing party and three others, at least they would have had Merritt whole and functioning. But he had listened to the arguments that with the Poohbears on strike, they couldn't spare Merritt; that even one-handed, they needed her.

And then *Tempest*. That had been a bad, bad world—fourteen members of the landing party, including Marlo and Raban, returning aboard ship with no obvious contamination, but slowly, over the next eight days, shivering themselves to death with an unknown, undiagnosable *something*, which leached the warmth from their bodies and finally the life as well. Three others, in spacesuits, returned to the ship and suffered the same fate. It had been Gilban who discovered the heat-trope, a submicroscopic virus; it had infected the second lot of three when they removed their spacesuits. The *Gypsy Moth* was out of fuel, they needed raw material for the converter or they would die in orbit around Tempest; it had been Gilban again who found the answer. The fuel-collecting crew had gone down in spacesuits, and then, returning, remained in the airlock, and in their suits, until *Gypsy Moth* had left orbit. Then, in the depths of interstellar space, they had been sent outside, for a "space walk" whose total, absolute-zero cold had killed the heat-trope infection on their suits, permitting them to return to the *Gypsy Moth* without infecting the crew.

Now *Gypsy Moth* had enough fuel for another few months of cruising—possibly a year, shiptime, at best.

Rae was saying, "We simply can't take the chance of setting down on another planet which might not be suitable for opening. We need children. We need fuel, and supplies. We need news of the Cosmos and the world-net——"

"Why?" Gildorric asked scornfully. "What are they to the Explorers?"

Gilrae said "Do you believe that we exist independently of the world-net? That we can go on forever without contact with them?"

"If need be," Gildorric said. "We are Explorers. It is our journey and our quest that makes us Explorers—not the worlds we find."

"He's right," Gilnosta said. "We can't crawl in, crippled, to any world that will have us, going begging to Head Centre for supplies and help to keep us going until we find another world! We're Explorers," she repeated proudly, "We go in as conquerors—or not at all!"

"It's an attractive mystique," Gilrae said, "unfortunately, it's only a mystique. And like all such mystiques, it's very far from the truth. Among other things, we need contact with the world-net and the world-lines of the Transmitter to let Head Centre know we're still alive and still searching. How many Explorer ships have simply vanished, without trace? Do we want to be written off too?"

Gildoran felt a sense of shock. You never spoke of that. Suddenly he wondered; had the other ships been destroyed? Or had they simply grown so full of their own lives out in Cosmos, so reluctant to interrupt their endless voyage with occasional touchdowns, that they had taken to the infinite reaches of space, abandoning any purpose in their voyage, remaining forever dissociated from planets and downworlders, spinning on their own axes in endless *hubris*. . . .

Gilrae said urgently "No! We need planets, just as the planets need *us!* We need contact with other Explorers. We need contact with other downworlders, we need *children*—we need it to keep us human! To keep us from forgetting *why* we're Explorers!" Her face was grim and decided. "I'm giving the bridge orders to set a course for the nearest charted, inhabited world. We set down there for overhaul, and to find out where the other Explorer ships are now."

She dismissed them and said no more, but Gildoran could guess what was in her mind. Cruelly short-handed as they were, the only hope now was to find another Explorer ship and combine their crews and forces.

Was this the last voyage of the *Gypsy Moth*, as herself? Were they simply too short-handed to go on? And what happened to an Explorer without a ship, when his long, long voyaging was done?

Wouldn't it be better to die in Cosmos, endlessly circling the long stars in an untouched, imperishable tomb, than to end their lives tied to downworld time, earthbound?

Gilrae was Captain again and she had the authority.

He was off duty for the moment, and had no wish to return to his own cabin, which he still shared with Gilmerritt—he had remained only because he feared, if he attempted to withdraw, that it might plunge her into deep depression. It was not an unwelcome arrangement entirely. Between her moments of depression, Merritt was a pleasant, companionable partner, and the strong sexual compatibility had never really disappeared.

There's no one I want more than Merritt. I suspect it's only the fact that I'm tied to her that makes me rebel against it.

He found that old habit was taking his feet to the furthest end of the living quarters, and into an empty room. There, surrounded by Gilramie's familiar things, he could relax and wait for her to come off-shift. He told himself he wouldn't wait for her, there was no need for that, he'd used her often enough as confidante and crying-towel during the bad year of his captaincy. But as usual, the stressless feel of her quarters relaxed him so much that he fell asleep, stretched out on her couch, and only the soft whirring of the opening door alerted him to Ramie's return.

He sat up, feeling a little dazed.

"I'm sorry, Ramie, I didn't mean . . . I'll go right away."

She laughed. "Why? You're not in my way, and I saw Merritt on the bridge, so she certainly won't be missing you.. What's on your mind, Gildoran?"

"Rae's decision to set down," Gildoran said. "You know we may never take off again. What would we do? What would happen to us, Ramie, if the *Gypsy Moth* never got off the ground again?"

She came and sat close to him on the couch. She still looked like a child—slender, almost breastless, her huge dark eyes serious and steady. She said, "I'd be sad, of course. But it wouldn't be the end of the world. It's a big Galaxy out there. There's sure to be somewhere I could go, something I could do somewhere."

"But . . . to be an earthworm . . . never to be an Explorer again. . . ."

Ramie said "There are other Explorer ships. If I felt that way, it would be Cosmos—not the *Gypsy Moth*—that would be important to me." Her smile trembled a little. "What would hurt would be losing you—all of you," she amended quickly. "But we'll worry about it when it happens. More likely, once we're downworld, we'll be able to modify the ship's computers and technology to operate with fewer personnel. At worst we can wait there until the children grow up a little—Gilmarina and Rita will be Class B in about two years—and everything will be all right."

Gildoran said, a little sourly, "Just a born optimist, aren't you?"

Ramie shrugged. "What did you want me to do? Tell you how hopeless it all was? I should think you'd get enough of that from Gilmerritt."

"You really dislike her, don't you? Or is it still only jealousy?"

"I don't dislike her. I *admire* her, for carrying on, even as well as she has done. It's outrageous, what she's had to go through. If I were crippled like that, I don't think I could carry on at all," Ramie said. "If anyone ever had a right to complain, she's the one. But it's been hard on you, too. As for being jealous . . ." another small shrug. "I'm used to it by now. Maybe it's just perversity. I only want what I can't have."

It's very strange. Ramie is closer to me than anyone alive. Why don't I love her as she wants me to? Why? Is there something wrong with me? She's certainly just as desirable as Gilmerritt. Maybe more so. And yet . . . and yet. . . .

It was several weeks of shiptime before the bridge crew called them together to tell them that they were in orbit around a great blue-white sun with three habitable planes, at least one of which had been technologically colonized.

"We've gotten Transmitter readings from it," Gilrae said. "We'll make contact and ask permission to set down. From there we can Transmit to Head Centre, or to Host, and make plans for the future."

Gildoran was working Communications when the first contact was made.

The voice on the panel sounded excited.

"The Explorer ship *Gypsy Moth?* We have heard nothing of any Explorer ships for twelve planetary years, but you are more than welcome to land here for repairs. It is our pleasure to offer you our hospitality. If you are not in dire emergency and can wait a few hours, a formal invitation will be extended to you from the Councillor. I have heard that the Councillor has a deep personal interest in the Explorer ships. If not, I am empowerd to grant you landing permission."

Gildoran replied that no, *Gypsy Moth* was shorthanded but not in desperate straits, and that they would be happy to wait for the Councillor's formal invitation.

"That's a relief," said Gillori. She was working as apprentice Navigator these days. "Suppose we'd set down on someplace where they hated the Explorers, like that world where they killed Gilmarin and almost killed you?"

"Lasselli's World? In that case," Gildoran said, "I suppose we'd just go on to the next star-system. But I'm glad we've found a place." He smiled at the girl. She was really a young woman now, he thought; she must be quite nineteen, and competent to hold any Major Office aboard *Gypsy Moth,* with the single exceptions of Transmitter and Medic Crew. Next time we draw for a Year-Captain, Lori will be on the list. It made Gildoran feel old.

It was less than a shiptime hour before the planet made contact again, this time to read out a formal invitation from the Councillor of Laszlo (that was as near as Gildoran could come, in Universal Phonetics, to the name) that the Explorer Ship *Gypsy Moth* was welcome to set down, giving them a choice of ports which had facilities to handle them, and extending an invitation to a formal reception for up to three dozen of the ship's personnel. Gildoran made the standard courteous reply and signed off, thinking with a faint grin, to get three dozen for an official reception, we'd have to bring along the children in Nursery and a couple of the Poohbears too!

At least they *had* the Poohbears. Between Hellworld and the Tempest, they hadn't had them, and after brutal, killing seven-hour shifts everyone aboard, from the Captain down to the children, had had to take extra shifts at baby-tending in Nursery and on the regrowth tank monitoring Gilmarina. Civilized man couldn't live at that pace, but they'd managed it somehow, until Tempest, when—without being asked—the Poohbears had come back to them.

Maybe on this world we can find some children. Although it's not certain we have the technicians for the necessary DNA operations any more.

It was the first time he'd been on the bridge for a ship-down. Last time the *Gypsy Moth* had been set down on a planet's surface, he'd been a Class-B, running errands. He'd been down in a landingcraft on Hellworld, but it wasn't the same. As, under Gildorric's direction, he and Lori piloted the enormous ship down to the port, he thought that in a few more years, everyone with any actual experience of landing an Explorer ship would be dead, or resigned to Floater status. You can do just so much with computers, on a strange planet. Downworld computers never bother to keep data for starship landing. The Explorer ships are the only ships there are—the colonized worlds used the Transmitters, they had no need of programs for a starship landing.

Ramie, who was off-shift, had brought Rita and Gilmarina to the bridge to watch the landing, something they may not see again for years. He was struck by how much Gilmarina looked like Ramie, now that her skin and hair were completely white. They had the same dark eyes with the epicanthic fold that gave them a long, slanting look, the same round smooth face, the delicate build and slender hands. Ramie came to Gildoran's side and said, "Remember what dear old Gilharrad said about planets—that the best worlds were found by ESP and hunches? I don't know why, but I feel *good* about this one. I think we're going to find what we want here."

He smiled at the young woman and said, "I hope you're right. Anyway, they're welcoming us. For the rest, we'll just have to wait and see."

II

Once they had landed, set up steps and unsealed the doors, they discovered that they had been guided down to a landing-space in a great open, flat, country, surrounded at a distance by low rings of mountains, not high, but rocky-red and flattened at their tops. The sun was dazzlingly blue-white and everywhere, vegetation grew lush and thickly.

"I'd expected a desert," Gildoran said, and Merritt replied "Not a chance. The tremendous amount of ultra-violet in the blue-white stars makes for lush plant growth."

It reminded Gildoran of something. Someplace strange and very long ago. The last planet he had seen had been Hellworld, and that certainly couldn't be it. The population of Laszlo was, like all worlds in the Transmitter world-net, enormously varied, all types and sizes and colors, but the predominant type, and therefore probably the indigenous or original colonizers, were of a single racial stock, tall, unusually dark-skinned, the majority well over six feet tall, even the women. . . .

Lasselli's World! Laszlo.

Was the name only a coincidence?

Somehow he didn't think so. Surrounded by the royal welcome which the inhabitants of Laszlo gave to *Gypsy*

155

Moth and her crew, it didn't seem important. If Lasselli's World and Laszlo were the same world, at least the political climate had changed and they were safe there. Safe? The Laszlans couldn't do enough for them!

For the first few days none of them did anything much except rest. The long, short-handed voyage had taken its toll of them all. Gildoran found himself seized by uncanny lassitude and the stress of gravity told more than he remembered. Ship's gravity, just strong enough to give them orientation and prevent vertigo, was something else entirely.

Several days later Gilrae came to his quarters and said, "Someone must take a trip to Host, and find out what's become of the rest of the Explorer fleet. I haven't the heart to put it off on anyone else. Will you come with me, Gildoran?"

"You're going by Transmitter?"

Rae said tartly, "Well, I'm certainly not going to take the *Gypsy Moth*."

"All right, I'll come." It had been a long time, Gildoran thought, since he had made a trip by Transmitter. Not since that strange trip with Ramie—how long ago? How old was Gilmarina now? Thirteen. Thirteen years, shiptime. It had been seven years since he had set foot on a planet, and then only those few disastrous days on Hellworld. He had escaped the Tempest disaster only because he'd been on Nursery duty that day.

As they walked through the great open land-bowl he felt the luxurious heat of the great sun beating on his back.

Feels good, to be on solid ground. The feel of that sun. I wonder how we survive, so long in space without sun or wind or the feel of gravity under our feet. . . . Man wasn't made to live in space.

He told himself sternly not to be sentimental. For him, gravity wasn't even a childhood imprint. He'd been picked up for an Explorer ship before he was a month old, and the retailoring of the very cell-print of his body, his very innermost cells, had been made, tailormade just for that—to live in space. He wasn't a planetman, an Earthworm, the differences were cell-deep, atom-deep. And yet . . . and yet, that sun, the cool sharp wind blowing against his cheek. . . .

He asked Gilrae, "Does it feel good to be on the surface again? Or are planets still just—what was it Gilharrad used to call them, just interruptions, holes in the Cosmos?"

"Dear, dear old Gilharrad," she said with a fond smile. "No, it feels good, but mostly because now I know you're all safe."

"Well, if we had to find a planet to set down on, permanently, we couldn't have found a better one," he said, then wondered exactly why he had said it as she raised a startled face to him. Did he mean that, would he want to stay here indefinitely?

There's a planet somewhere with your name on it. . . .

He had the uncomfortable sensation that Gilrae could follow what he was thinking, but she forebore to say anything, simply asking, as they approached the Transmitter terminal, "Have you ever been on Host? I wish we could have gone directly there. But it's almost fifty light-years from here; I don't think *Gypsy Moth* could have made it."

"If I was ever there, it was when I was too young to remember," Gildoran said.

"It's the home world of the Explorers," Gilrae said, "as much of a home world as they have. All our stored data

157

is there. I have a transcript of *Gypsy Moth*'s log with me, for the Archives-Major store." As they stepped into a Transmitter booth, she said "It's a good thing we put in. Our Transmitters are obsolete. I'll have to send Gilmarti over for briefing on the new models. It seems the old four-light-years limit has been pushed out. These can handle twelve LYs without damage or disorientation."

She touched a set of co-ordinates, and there was a brief, sharp sense of whirling darkness, a small electrical *snap,* and the console before them had changed from blue to green and after repeating the maneuver twice more, they stood on Host.

It was a small planet, so small that it seemed to Gildoran, as he stood under the twilit grey canopy that was Host's sky, that he could see and feel the swift rotation, the rapid motion of the little planetoid abou its dim and faraway sun. Or was that simply an illusion based on the swift overhead passing of some heavenly bodies which could have been moons or elaborate artificial satellites? It was cold, even through the thick warm Travel Cloaks with which they had provided themselves on Laszlo.

As they left the Transmitter terminal—it was a small one, Host evidently had little transient travel—a line of assorted humanoids stepped back before the Explorers.

Marked out. Alien. You would only have noticed it if they hadn't.

But then he saw the expressions on their faces. Not fear or hatred, this time—respect, verging on awe. And then the tall quasi-uniformed female at the head of their line said in a clear, carrying, perhaps mechanically amplified voice, "Please form into an orderly line and we will commence our tour with an inspection of the Explorer museum. . . ." and he understood.

Gilrae lifted an eyebrow at him and said, "That's new. Last time I was here we were fighting to keep our allotment from being disallowed. For centuries—since before I was born—we've had a small subsidy from Head Centre for locating new planets. But then I remember Head Centre was trying to cut us down—they said that if we couldn't make enough on finder's fees to support our own ships we should get out of the business. Two or three ships actually *did* go broke and had to decommission." She was smiling, a little tremulously. "I was prepared to find, when we downworlded this time, that we'd been entirely disallowed, and Host had closed up shop. There was some talk then—I don't know how many centuries ago planetary time—that there had been enough planets discovered for the foreseeable future, and that the Explorers were just a luxury the civilized Galaxy couldn't afford—siphoning off money and energy to a frontier. Time we settled down, they said, and learned to live on the worlds we had."

She paused for a moment before a small carven memorial. Two figures carved in some alabaster-white metal, pale and elongated and obviously of Explorer type, stood triumphantly on a small jade-green planet. It was the first time Gildoran had ever seen a public inscription in the language the Explorers used among themselves. There was a translation into Universal ideographs below. Both inscriptions read:

> TO THE CREW OF THE *SEA WOLF*
> LOST IN A NOVA IN THE VICINITY
> OF THE NEBULA IN ORION.
> 'To strive, to seek, to find, and not to yield.'

"That's new too," Rae said, "or should I say—since my

time. I've no idea how long it's been, planet time, since I was last here."

There was a small building whose doorway said—again in the language the Explorers used, *Authorized and Ship's Personnel Only.* Gilrae pressed her ident disk against the sensitive plate on the door and it opened.

Before a computer console, a tall pale Explorer was seated; he turned as they came in. "Gilrae of *Gypsy Moth,*" he said warmly, turning. "We heard the report of your surfacing. We were afraid you'd been lost in space, my dear."

"Sarndall of *Spray,*" Gilrae said, and embraced the strange man warmly. She introduced Gildoran, who felt strangely ill at ease. It was the first time he had ever met anyone who was so obviously one of them, an Explorer, and yet not one of his own. He didn't know how to act with the stranger who was not a stranger.

Gilrae asked "Where *is* Spray now, Dall? Or shouldn't I ask?"

"Downworlded and decommissioned," Sarndall said, "Three successive lots of children all died, and we became too short-handed to go on; and we lost our Poohbears in an epidemic; seven of them died in one night. We were too disheartened to try to go out again. Fortunately there was work for most of us here on Host."

"Is the news all bad?"

"Not all, though it's not good. You saw the monument to *Sea Wolf?* But *Tinkerbelle* just surfaced, and they have four new planets opened and eight healthy four-year-olds growing up. And how is it with you, Rae?"

"Not good," Gilrae said, and gave the old Explorer the log transcript. "The details are in this." She gave him a brief account of the Hellworld and Tempest disasters.

"Lethal soundwaves from plants, eh? That's a new one," Sarndall said. "I'll file it in the list of dangers.

We've met that cold-death thing before in that same sector, I think; maybe ships should be warned out of that sector for a few thousand years until it exhausts all possible hosts and dies out. Of course the computer people will make that decision in the long run, but it's worth thinking about. So you're not opening a planet now?"

"No, we had to make a forcedown. We're on Laszlo."

"Good place for Explorers," Sarndall said. "Funny thing about Laszlo. For sixty years planet time, they were on the warn-off list. About a hundred and nineteen years ago we had a report of an Explorer mobbed and killed there, so we put out warnings. Then, about thirty years ago, they chose a new government—President, King, I forget what nonsense they call their leader——"

"Councillor," Gildoran murmured.

"Something like that. Anyway, his first official act was to get in touch with Host and open Laszlo formally to Explorers. They have a few special projects there that would interest you, I suspect."

"I imagine we'll find out about them," Gilrae said. "We're invited to a formal reception there. Up to three dozen of us. We'll have to take everybody down to the Poohbears to make up that number!"

"So bad?" Sarndall answered.

"We're thinking of decommissioning," Rae said frankly. "That bad."

Sarndall's eyes were suddenly greedy. "Don't do that," he begged, "If it's a manpower problem, let us join on. There are twenty-nine of us, all dying to get out into Cosmos again. . . ."

"It's a thought," Gilrae said, "but of course the decision isn't mine. It would be up to the whole crew."

As they were leaving Host again, waiting in line behind the tourists who had completed their tour of the Explorer museum for the single Transmitter booth, Gildoran said, "That could be the solution to the manpower problem, Rae."

"Maybe." But Rae looked grave. "It almost never works," she said. "It's been tried. But it makes for two factions aboard a ship; *us* and *them*. We're not a family any more. Not a single crew all of whom think of *Gypsy Moth* as our own special single home, but two crews. Each trying to run the ship its own way. It might, as a last resort, be better than trying to decommission. But not much better."

Gildoran, too, had felt the strangeness; to be with an Explorer who both was and was not one of his own. All his life, since he was able to speak, every Explorer he had ever known was one of his own crew—his shipmate, his nurserymate, his own family; to be loved, protected, defended against the entire Cosmos, against every other being in Cosmos. Everyone who was *not* one of *Gypsy Moth's* crew was an alien, a stranger, who could never understand. . . . Even those you thought you loved, like Janni, never really knew you, or cared to.

Except for that boy—what was his name? Merrik—on Lasselli's World. He had suddenly become a friend—and then he had had to say goodbye again.

And then, suddenly, he visualized the familiar halls, rooms and decks of *Gypsy Moth* filled with strangers. Explorers, yes. Part of the crew. But not—oh, no, never brothers, crewmates. Never known, beloved. Of them and yet not of them. Strangers and not strangers. Alien and not alien. Gildoran shuddered.

Cosmos forbid!

He watched Rae programming the coordinates for Laszlo, and a random memory flickered in his mind, a memory of strange coordinates etched into an override signal . . . one unforgettable day in his youth.

Laszlo. Lasselli's World. Strange and the same, yet different beyond recognition. As they stepped out into the fierce blue-white dayshine, stormy with colorless clouds and the flicker of lightning in the upper atmosphere, he heard himself say, "Home again." He corrected himself quickly, back to *Gypsy Moth,* which was home, but that was not what he meant, and Rae's surprised eyes, raised to his, knew it.

He said "Did you know this was Lasselli's World, Rae?"

"Yes, I knew. I didn't know you did."

"Gilmarin was killed here."

And I'm calling it home!

"I know," Rae said quietly. "And I was born here. No one knew except Gilharrad, and he's dead. He lost his finger when he stole me—and three others—from here. And it was for that, I suspect, for the memory of that raid that Gilmarin died." She drew her travel cloak closely about her. "The place gives me the creeps. Do you mind if we go back on board *Gypsy Moth* right away?"

III

During the next few days Gildoran explored the down-world with Gilmarina, enjoying her first uninhibited taste of sunshine and freedom. Ramie, or occasionally Gilmerritt, sometimes accompanied them on these excursions, and when he saw family groups enjoying themselves in the green parks of Laszlo, he realized that a family was less a biological unit than a functional one. In every way that mattered, he and Ramie were Gilmarina's parents.

Gilmerritt was a little hesitant about showing herself on the surface. In this day and age, a deformity like her crippled hand was truly astonishing, and people stared sometimes. She was appallingly sensitive about it, and Gildoran didn't blame her.

He broached the subject to her, in their shared quarters aboard *Gypsy Moth*, one night. "There's no reason you can't go into a growth tank any time now, Merritt. There is an excellent regrowth center here. And we will be here at least a year, waiting for the children to grow up. We wouldn't leave you anyway."

"I know," Merritt said, "I visited the growth center the other day."

"Then shall we make the arrangements soon?"

Merritt shook her head. "Not yet," she said, "I have work to do. I want to do some research there."

He looked at her in astonishment. She said seriously

"Do you mind, Gildoran? I . . . first, I don't want to be away from you so long. And besides . . . there's something special I have to do. But do you really mind? Are you . . . are you ashamed to be seen with . . . with this?" She raised the blackened, useless claw.

Gildoran drew her close. "Darling, don't even think of that. I'd love you if you had no hands at all. But . . ." he shook his head, faintly bewildered. "For so long, it's the only thing you've wanted——"

"People tend to lose their sense of perspective, sometimes," Merritt said slowly. "Just now I think there's something more important. Do you mind, Doran?"

He said, holding her tightly in his arms, "You must do what seems best to you, my love." Here on this new world, where everything seemed new and fresh and somehow more real than in their isolated world between the stars, he was becoming freshly aware of how deeply and dearly he cherished her, how he would miss her if she were away from him so long. He found himself almost selfishly glad that they need not be separated. And yet he wondered what it could be that seemed so important to her that she would delay further the regeneration of her crippled hand. She did not offer to tell him, and he did not ask. He saw her poring over technological and medical journals, and she spent a great deal of time at the regrowth center, but he did not know why. She had always spent a great deal of time in reading and studying her chosen specialties—he suspected that in time she would have switched from the biological crew to the Medic crew—but until they landed here, he had somehow felt that her obsessive interest in regrowth techniques was, at least in part, a way to make him feel guilty for the delay in salvaging her hand. Now he knew it was not that—but what could it be?

He accused her once, almost teasingly, "I suspect you

want Gilban's job some day. Chief Medic Gilmerritt?" and she laughed and did not deny it, but that was all.

She was at the conference, too, where the Major Officers met to discuss acquiring some more children. The Poohbears, having no little ones left in Nursery, were all in favor of it. Gilmerritt's was the first voice raised against it.

"I think we must wait," she said. "We are going to be here at least a year, perhaps more. We cannot make the DNA modification until shortly after we take off. With the techniques we are using now, the child must be raised in free fall and deep space to develop the full Explorer mutation. If we take newborn or new-hatched infants now, they will be too old for the DNA change by the time we leave here."

Gilrae glanced at the chief Medic. "Gilban?"

"With our present technology, Merritt is right," he said. "I heard on Host that the *Spray,* bring short-handed, took a group of five-year-olds, hoping to diminish the time before they would be old enough to work ship. Not a single one survived."

Gilrae said quietly "We needn't wait. I promised to put it to you. The crew of the *Spray* wants to join us—and there are twenty-nine of them. This would give us a crew of more than sixty. We could be off again next month, if we wished—with a crew of children for the Nursery—and be fully operational again for the first time in years.

To the murmur of voices—half approving, half in protest—that rose at once, she raised a hand. "We don't have to decide now," she said, "It must be put to vote. Think it over. We'll call another meeting and decide. But remember before you decide that the alternative is probably decommissioning. The Councillor's formal reception is tonight. It's not compulsory, but the Laszlans have been very kind to us, so please don't absent yourselves without some good reason."

Ramie caught up with him in the corridor. "Doran, did you hear this about the *Spray?* You didn't look particularly surprised when Rae brought it up."

"I heard it on Host," Gildoran said.

"It could be the answer," Ramie said. "We could all stay together, that way."

"But strangers—on *Gypsy Moth* . . ."

"They wouldn't be strangers. They're Explorers. Like us."

"It would be better if they *were* strangers," Gildoran said helplessly, "We could learn to adapt to them—and they to us—as we do when we're downworld. But the crew of another Explorer ship—with its own traditions—of us and still not of us—I honestly don't think it would work, Ramie."

"No, not if it split us into warring factions," Ramie said. "I see your point. I've often thought the perfect solution would be to be able to sign on adult volunteers whenever we needed them. Then there wouldn't be so much *difference* between Explorers and downworld people. We wouldn't be freaks to them, and they wouldn't be alien races to us. It wouldn't be any more of a difference than transferring from Nursery to Transmitter Crew. We'd all just be *people* together." She considered a moment, her pretty pale face pensive. "Maybe we could do that with another Explorer crew. But it would be hard, because we'd expect them to be just like us. And they *couldn't* be." She sighed and shook her head. "Well, maybe the right answer will turn up."

"If we have to join with the *Spray*," Gildoran said harshly, "I'll go earthworm! Better live here among strangers I *know* are strangers, than try to pretend they're not."

Ramie looked startled and shocked. "Could you do that to us, Gildoran?"

He turned away, saying harshly "I wouldn't be the first, and I won't be the last."

He thought about that as he was pulling himself, with an ill grace, into dress clothes for the Councillor's formal reception.

Maybe I would be the last. What did they say on Host—that perhaps they were going to cut off the Explorer ships? Well, I'm sure the Cosmos will survive very nicely without them, for the next few million years at least. By then, maybe they'll have something better.

Gilmerritt, in a slim green sheath the color of her eyes, stepped up behind him. "You're going to the Councillor's reception?"

"I don't suppose I could get out of it," Gildoran said. "Rae asked everyone to go. Aren't you?"

"I'd rather not. But I will, if you're going," she said. "Who is the Councillor?"

"How would I know? Some important politician, I suppose, who has a thing about Explorers. I don't know whether he romanticizes us, or whether he just wants to know whether we really do kill and eat the children we steal or buy."

Gilmerritt made an expressive face of disgust. "Are there really people who still believe that?"

"Merritt, there are people who will believe *anything*," Gildoran said.

"Then maybe we'd better take Gilmarina with us. To prove otherwise," Gilmerritt said, and Gildoran shrugged. "If she wants to go, I'm perfectly willing. But it seems a shame. She's really too young to have to be let in for these wretched formal affairs."

Gildoran found Gilmarina with Rae, playing a tall electronic harp in one of the Recreation rooms. Marina had recently been released officially from the Nursery and had a room of her own, which she shared with Gilrita.

The Nursery's empty now. Strange how dead the Ship feels without babies aboard. And the children are the only future we have.

Gildoran stood, silent and unmoving, listening to the woman and the girl playing an elaborate duet. It was Gilrae who saw him first and broke off in the middle of an arpeggio.

"I see you're dressed for the Councillor's reception. Shall we all go together, then?"

Gilmarina looked astonished and delighted. "Can I really go, Rae?"

"Of course, darling, if you want to," Rae said, and Gilmarina smiled. She had deep dimples in each cheek. "I'd better go and dress! I can imagine that it would hardly be protocol to turn up in Ship uniform!"

Gilmerritt laughed. "I doubt if the Laszlans would know the difference," she said, "they surely don't expect us to know, or abide by, their dress codes. Dress codes follow such subliminal cues anyhow. In worlds with the Transmitter, I doubt if anyone pays much attention any more. But it must have been a full-time occupation, to stay appropriately dressed, in the days when that was an important consideration."

"It was," Gilrae said. "I spent my twenties helping open up a world which became a pleasure resort, and it amused me to learn something about the psychology of appropriate dress there, and to compare it with the other

169

worlds I visited. Of course, on a pleasure-world it's a deliberate thing—and quite artificial."

"Isn't it artificial everywhere?" Merritt asked. "Except, that is, on world with extremes of climate, where you'd freeze or get sunstroke in the wrong clothing?"

"I don't know," Gilrae said. "It's a matter of subtle cues given and received, and if you give the wrong ones for the society, you may be in trouble."

"I imagine that's why Travel Cloaks were invented," Gildoran said. "Imagine an ordinary woman on one planet going out for a day's shopping, stepping just a few light-years away for something a little different to wear, and discovering she's suddenly subject—in her ordinary house-dress—to being sexually accosted."

Gilmerritt shrugged. "I'm sure it happens," she said, "but unless she's terribly neurotic, surely she wouldn't mind. She could always say no, or pretend not to understand his language."

Gilmarina returned, in close-fitting tights and a brief flared tunic of brilliant crimson, her pale hair tied into a glittered scarf.

She's a woman, and a pretty one. But she's still a baby, to me. She always will be.

The women admired Gilmarina's dress and they all started down toward the Transmitter. Gildoran was wearing ordinary dress uniform, silver and blue—the Councillor, confound him, wanted them not as guests but specifically as Explorers, so why not? Rae, as befitted an Elder, wore pale draperies, with artificial snowflakes in her snowy hair. Gilmerritt, in her green sheath, and Gilmarina in her brilliant tunic, were pretty women who might have come from any world of the millions who surrounded them.

"I suppose any attention to dress will wear off in a few years," Gilrae said, as they set the Transmitter coordinates for the destination of the Councillor's Residence, "No one alive could possibly learn all those subliminal cues for more than one or two planets—four or five, if anyone wanted to make it a lifetime study or specialty."

"And what a waste of time," Gilmerritt laughed, as the brief sparkling darkness surrounded them.

Do we go through the Transmitter all together? Are we somehow intermingled, atoms mixing in the interspace between the Terminals. How do we know. that each of us gets our own flesh and blood back? Am I part of everyone I've ever shared a Transmitter booth with?

He briefly considered signing up for Transmitter crew on their next voyage. But the possibility that the *Gypsy Moth* might never take another voyage caused black depression to settle down on him like a blanket.

"You don't look very festive, Gildoran." Gilrae slid her arm through his. "This is a party. Cheer up!"

He didn't feel at all festive. But for Gilrae's sake he let a smile cover his face like a mask.

"I'll do my best," he said. "I imagine that must be the Councillor's Residence over there, with all the lights and floating balloons around it. I'm glad it's not far—this must be in the Polar regions!"

They crossed the paved square through lightly falling snow, and went into the brightly-lit Official Residence.

IV

What Gilrae had said about clothes could equally well apply to entertainments, Gildoran thought as they paused in the outer, marbled hall of the Residence to be divested of their Travel Cloaks by noiselessly moving servomechanisms. Formality in some places was random informality in another. An official reception on one world might mean that you stood quietly in line and listened to speeches by dignitaries; on another it might mean that you lolled about on cushions and sang drinking songs. It had been years since Gildoran had attended any formal entertainment—or for that matter had mixed in large groups except with his own shipmates.

The most formal thing I've attended in thirteen years is the yearly Captain-choosing.

He murmured something of this to Rae as they went below lines of overhead crystal chandeliers, and she nodded. "Some day—any millennia now," she said, "some group or other will attempt to create guides for intercosmic etiquette. I believe they have something like that already but only in high diplomatic interplanetary political circles. When customs gets homogenized all the way down the social scales, decadence starts." She chuckled a little. "But as long as the Explorers keep opening up new worlds, decadence can be indefinitely delayed. Maybe we're the little leaven that leavens the whole Galaxy."

"Citizens of Laszlo and Honored Guests," the abnormally sweet, mechanical voice of a servomech proclaimed, "The ship's officers of the Explorer ship *Gypsy Moth*. Gildoran; Gilrae; Gilmarina; Gilmerritt."

A fat little woman close to them murmured audibly "Oh, they're the Explorers! Councillor Marik is simply mad on the subject, you know!" She smiled up sweetly at Gildoran and asked "Could you tell me, why your names are all so much alike?"

Gildoran couldn't see that their names all were that much alike, but he replied courteously, explaining that every Explorer ship had a specific coded identification which was made into a single syllable—*Gil* in the case of *Gypsy Moth*—and given as the first syllable of the name of every person on that ship, so that from the name of the Explorer, any Explorer in the fleet could immediately identify him by the ship he came from.

"And how many ships are there in the Explorer fleet?" the woman asked.

"I really couldn't say. Perhaps Gilrae could tell you," Gildoran said, carefully not looking at the other woman.

Another man in the crowd around them said, "The ships have such strange and romantic names. Where do they come from?"

"The ships? Most of them were built on Host," Gildoran replied.

"No, the names! Where do the names come from?"

"They are names of ships sailed by explorers on mankind's original world," Gildoran replied, "or at least that's what the legends say. *Ships* were a form of land transit, I believe, and in those days explorers went out to find out all they could about their own world before they went into space. The names of some of those ships have been preserved in legend, or as far as we know that is true. Of course, after so many years, who can tell?"

A servomechanism glided up to him and attracted his attention by a discreet tug at his uniform sleeve.

"Gildoran of the *Gypsy Moth?* Councillor Marik wishes to speak to you personally, if you will be so good," it murmured.

Just about the last thing Gildoran wanted was to go and chat with some higher-up political biggie who romanticized the Explorers, but he couldn't think of a single polite way to refuse. He followed the servomech to the Councillor's raised thronelike chair.

Councillor Marik was a shivelled little figure, dark-skinned, but his hair was white as Gildoran's own. He looked up as Gildoran came close, and said:

"You don't remember me, do you, Gildoran? No, how could you, after—how many years has it been? More than a hundred, for me. You said you wouldn't come back, because I'd be sure to hate you. . . ."

Something in the voice touched a string of memory in Gildoran. He said "Merrikl" with a curious sense of warmth.

Was this why I felt this world was home, because I found a friend here I would never forget?

"You don't shoot escaped snakes in the forestry preserve any more, then?"

The old man chuckled. "You *do* remember, then. As for you—it's true, you don't look a day older. No, I take that back," he said, scanning the other man's face. "What's happened? I understand your ship's in trouble. But it's good to have you as a guest here."

It was with a curious sense of things falling into place that Gildoran took a seat beside the Councillor and began to tell him what had befallen the *Gypsy Moth* in the years between.

If I choose to stay here as an earthworm, at least I shall begin with a friend. Not wholly as a stranger, then. And a friend, after all, in high places. Certainly I shall be able to find something worthwhile here.

Marik listened to Gildoran's tale in silence, seeming fascinated. Finally, when he heard of the choice facing them—to join with another Explorer ship or decommission—he said seriously, "But that is terrible! Not that you wouldn't be welcome here, any or all of you. But every Explorer ship we lose——"

"Even Head Centre seems to think we're a luxury the Galaxy can dispense with," Gildoran said.

"Head Centre likes playing God," Marik said, "but this thing is too big for politics on this scale. I don't think you realize what the Explorers mean to us, Gildoran. You're too close to the problem—what's the old saying, you can't see the Ocean for the surf?"

Gildoran said "I'd be curious to know what you think the Explorers mean. To most of the people of most planets, we're either freaks, or a dangerous strangeness, a legend people hate."

"You're our safety valve," Marik said. "Our permanent frontier, our endless open end. As long as the Explorers are finding and opening new worlds, we can all be different, keep our individuality. Once the discovery of new worlds ends, once everything is known, we begin to stagnate; we begin to die. It's like a race gone sterile; with nothing new beginning, that race, or that world, begins to die. When life is simply repeating the known, when nothing new enters the equation, we find first a loss of new ideas, then of creativity in general, then general decadence. It's happened, historically, to every new planet when it's been entirely explored and mapped; from that moment it begins to die and go decadent. Man can't live, psychologically, without a frontier. And even if we—all of us—can't go exploring, we can survive, psychologically, knowing that new worlds *are* being found, that *someone* can go and find them."

It reminded him, a little, of what Gilrae had been saying—about homogenizing of manners being the beginning of decadence. But he asked, bitterly, "Why do so many people ban us from their worlds, then? Why do they deny us children?"

"Because they don't understand," Marik said quietly. "I've spent my life, Gildoran, trying to make sure that Laszlo will understand. I think you'll find you can have all the children you want, here." He smiled a little wistfully and said "I myself would be happy to know that someone of my blood would be exploring the stars, a thousand years after my old bones were dust. And I'm sure there are millions who feel just as I do. Here and elsewhere."

That would be the answer, perhaps, Gildoran thought as the crew of the *Gypsy Moth* left the Residence much later that night, and walked toward the Transmitter Terminal. A world where the Explorers were not freaks and hated aliens, but an Explorer homeworld, where they could come each time they opened a new world; where they could return for their children instead of buying or stealing, where every family on this planet had a child on the Explorer ships—and if Head Centre chose to close down Host, and phase out their support of the Explorers, Laszlo could remain as their home base. . . .

But as they entered the Transmitter he turned and said to Gilrae, "Take the girls home, will you? I'm going out for a while——"

"I'll go with you," Gilmerritt said, "unless you really want to be alone."

"I think I do. Thank you, darling, but you go home with Gilmarina. I'll see you tomorrow."

He stepped into a booth and pressed the coordinates for the main Transmitter Terminal on Laszlo. Here, in this terminal, he and Ramie had nearly been killed. Now they were honored guests.

He went outside, into the cool soft night. Laszlo was at a central location in the Galaxy and the night was brilliant with thousands upon thousands of close-in, brilliant stars. It seemed to him that from the surface of this world the stars were somehow brighter than ever in space, that the soft winds and clouds touched his body with a warmth he had never known.

I don't want to leave this world again. No matter how many worlds I see, there will never be another world which is mine, in this curious inexplainable sense. If I leave Laszlo, it will be tearing myself out by the roots, never to be whole again.

All that night, and all the following day, Gildoran went from Transmitter to Transmitter, jumping around the planet, from dayside to nightside, walking in the sun and rain, in park and desert, beauty spot and stinking slum, trying to find some part of Laszlo which he could honestly leave.

It was night again when he returned to the *Gypsy Moth,* sleepless, hungry, his eyes aching and his heart heavy. When he boarded and pressed his ident disk against the lock, the computer said "Gildoran, urgent you report to Recreation Area One. Ship's Council is about to convene, and Gilrae has been trying to locate you for hours."

177

When he came up to the area, he had half expected to find the whole ship's company assembled and was astonished to find only Gilrae there.

She raised her eyes, with a look of relief so great that he thought for a moment that she would burst into tears.

"Gildoran," said she. "I was afraid you had gone for good——"

"If I went it would not be for good," Gildoran said.

"For good or ill, then," Rae said wearily. "You are thinking of deserting, aren't you?"

"I wouldn't say that, exactly. But I'm uncertain about what's ahead. And uneasy."

How had she known?

As if she read his thoughts, as Gilrae so often did, she raised her eyes and said, "There's a look they get, when a world takes hold on them. You have it. I can't imagine why—a world like this one, it gives me the creeps. But then, no one except the one it's happened to can ever explain it. I saw it with Giltallen, for months before he left us. And now you. . . ." Her face twisted as if she were about to cry.

"Don't, Rae. I'm here."

"But for how long?"

He wanted to make a quick promise, but then, meeting Rae's eyes, he knew that with her, at least, he could only be completely honest. He said "It depends mostly on what happens in Ship's Council, Rae. I can't live with our joining the *Spray*."

"Ramie told me you felt like that," Rae said quietly. "Do you dislike them all so much?"

"It's not that I dislike them. I don't *know* them," Gildoran said. "Better a strange world than my own world suddenly made strange——"

"Even if the cost is leaving all of us?" Rae said. "I can't imagine what Ramie—or Gilmarina—would do without you. And as for me . . ." she leaned back against him, with a sigh. "But I certainly don't have to tell you what you mean to me, Doran, it's the one thing I'm sure you know. And I know you're not doing this just to make trouble. I know how you must feel. I know it all too well. . . ."

He held her in his arms, knowing Rae was dearer to him than anyone alive. But she understood and he knew she wouldn't fight him, whatever he wanted to do. . . .

He loosed her as others of the *Gypsy Moth's* company began to come into the room, one by one. Ramie cast a bitter look at him, as she came in. She said, "So you've come back again? Did you come to blackmail us into settling things your way? You know we can't lose you, and still go on."

Gildoran said quietly "That's not fair, Ramie. Every one of us has a right to a free choice. You will choose your way no matter what I do. I could try to talk you into staying with me, you know."

Ramie flared "And if you did—wouldn't that be a kind of blackmail too? Trying to get me to choose your way, just because you know how long I've loved you? Yes, I do love you. No one else has ever meant anything to me. There's been no one else for me, there never will be."

"Now who's trying blackmail?" Gildoran flared. He did not know whether the wild uprush of emotion he felt was love, or desire, or pure hatred. "You could have anyone you wanted!"

"You don't have to rub it in. I know that you don't care anything for me!" Ramie almost shouted at him.

Gilrae said wearily "Ramie. Doran. This is . . . this is unseemly."

"We're not in Nursery and we're not quarreling like

babies," Ramie said, turning viciously on the older woman. "You've no right, Rae! It's easy enough for you to talk, when you know that every man on *Gypsy Moth* loves you first and never after cares for anyone else——"

"Ramie! Ramie!" Gilrae said, in honest shock. "How can you say such things?"

"Ask Gildoran if it isn't true! Ask him if he's ever really loved anyone else—"

Gildoran rose in anger, swinging around to face both of the women. He said brutally "Damn all women! I wish I'd never come back, to listen to this! You're like a pack of jackals!"

Ramie stood facing him, angrily, tears pouring down her cheeks. Gilrae buried her head in her hands, and her shoulders were shaking. Gildoran was appalled but after a minute he realized, and was shocked to see, that she was laughing.

Ramie looked shocked, too, when Gilrae raised her head and she saw the other woman's laughter. Gilrae said "I must be really getting old. This just seems funny to me. But, both of you. . . ." she stretched her hands to them, and Gildoran saw, with shock, that although she was laughing, her thin lined hands were trembling.

"Doran. Ramie. Whatever happens with either of you, don't go into it like this. Don't settle it in a storm of emotion. It may be the last thing that ever happens to all of us as one. After today it will be too late, and it may affect the Explorers—not just *Gypsy Moth;* all that are left of us. You can't let an . . . an emotional flareup destroy all of us. Think it over and try to decide. . . ." she broke off. "I won't say, *decide without emotion.* It's an emotional decision. I realize that, perhaps more than any of you. God knows I feel emotional enough about it. But try and decide what you really want—what you'll want, not today, but months from now. Years from now. And decide so it won't be too late."

The other crew members were coming in now, taking seats all over the room. Gildoran slid into a seat, and suddenly realized that he was sitting exactly where he had been sitting when seven or eight years ago he had been chosen Captain. It seemed a lifetime ago. It *was* a lifetime ago. Ramie started to slip into a seat beside him; gave him an angry glare and moved to another. Had Rae tried to locate her, too?

Briefly Rae explained the choice that faced them. They were too short-handed to work *Gypsy Moth* for another thirteen or fourteen years shiptime until another crew of babies could grow up to help them. Their choices were either to decommission *Gypsy Moth* and disband the crew, or to join forces with the crew of the *Spray*, creating one ship's crew from two.

"Each of you has a vote, from the oldest Floater to the youngest child," Rae explained quietly. "It is your future, too. A majority will decide. I should state also that if a majority votes to decommission, or to join *Spray*, the vote will be binding on the minority. We will vote from eldest to youngest. Gildorric?"

"Join *Spray*," the old man said briefly, "I wouldn't live three planet-years in gravity. I just hope I live long enough for us to get free of the planet again."

"Gilmarti?"

"Decommission," she said. "Better an earthworm than try to mix with another crew."

"Gilban?"

The Chief Medic frowned and said "Abstain. I'll go with the majority, whatever you decide."

The voting went on. Gildoran tried to keep count but could not. When Gilramie's name was called she said, "Join with *Spray*. The time might come when we could separate out again, if there were enough of us, some day. But it means keeping the Explorers alive."

Gildoran knew he was next on the roster. Gilrae's face was haggard, almost desperate, as she said, "Gildoran."

My life is here.

The call of a world, a world I've made my own. And yet . . . how could I cut myself off from Ramie, even if all we do is quarrel? She's part of my life. From Merritt, who's so much mine, who has needed me so much—from Marina, whose very life came from me. . . .

"Gildoran?"

To share the Gypsy Moth, day by day, year by year, world by world and century, with strangers . . . strangers trying to be part of us. . . .

He saw Ramie's white face, twisted in anguish. He opened his mouth to say, "Decommission," and the words would not come. He said at last, fighting the syllables through a dry throat, "Abstain. I'll go with the majority. It's a case of lesser evil, either way."

Rae's chest heaved, as if she was struggling to breathe.

He wanted to speak, to burst into a flood of explanation, but Rae had called the next name.

"Gilbarni?"

"Join with *Spray*," the boy said, "Explorers are explorers. No planet's worth staying on."

I felt that way once. . . .

"Gillori?"

Lori's round face was pale and frightened. She said "I vote to decommission."

"Gilrita?"

The other of the "babies" said, so faintly hat she could hardly be heard, "I vote to join *Spray*. We could use some new friends."

"Gilmarina?"

Gilmarina murmured "I'll . . ." she looked pleadingly at Gildoran and said faintly "I'll abstain. I don't really know enough about it to vote. I'll agree to whatever the majority does."

Gilrae bent over the tally of the votes. Gildoran waited, hardly able to breathe. The next few moments would decide the fate of all of them. Some people might have been keeping an accurate count. He envied them. They already knew, without this murderous suspense. . . . he wished he had the courage to get up and walk out, into the sunlight of Laszlo, into the world he had sworn should be his, the world with his name on it, his special island. . . .

Gilmerritt rose and said "Rae, this wasn't necessary. If I may speak——"

Someone shouted, "Give us the results of the vote!"

Gilmerritt said "I tallied them. There were ten votes to join *Spray;* ten to decommission, and three abstentions. There is no vote, and we need no vote." Her face was pale. She held up her useless, claw-like hand. "I have been studying regrowth and DNA techniques," she said. "For obvious reasons. Our techniques are obsolete. With the new medical techniques at the command of the Laszlans," she said, "there is no reason we cannot sign on adult volunteers. I won't go into the technology involved," she added. "No one but Gilban and Gilnosta would understand it. But in general it's a matter of bone-marrow regeneration. with transplants and DNA transfusions. This means that anyone beneath a certain age—actually the age when bone growth is complete and the epiphyses sealed—can sign on to an Explorer ship. There will be no need for taking children as babies—although we may still wish to, because one of our greatest pleasures is to see them grow up as a part of our world—but the adult volunteer, with a few minor surgical modifications, and a few weeks now and then in a regrowth tank, can perfectly well survive the journey into deep interstellar space. We might still choose to join forces—for a time —with people from the *Spray*," she added, "but it is no longer a question of two separate factions. We will all be different—and equal," she ended. "It will take time to teach the newcomers the ways of the ship. But already, on Laszlo, Councillor Marik has found us three dozen volunteers. We can go whenever we will," she finished, "and we will always have a home base here on Laszlo. Whatever new world we find, we will come back here, for new crew members, for children, for a world which will always be our own home world," she finished, before her words were drowned out in an outburst of wild cheering.

V

"After this year," Gilrae said, "I'm applying for Floater status. But whether I get it or not, I'm finished. This is my last term as Captain."

Ramie laughed and said "I've heard *that* before, too."

Rae said "Wait till *you've* been Captain a time or two and see how you feel about it."

Gilmerritt said "I've better things to occupy my time. Speaking of which, I'd better get down to the Medic area and see that the tanks are all ready for null-grav conditions. How are the volunteers making out on the bridge, Rae?"

The woman looked around. "As well as any other Class-B crew," she said. "After six months of intensives, what did you expect?" She smiled affectionately at Gilmarina, bent over a Communications console, looking tense and a little scared. She said "Give me shipwide hookup, Marina—All Hands attention, this is the Captain. *Gypsy Moth* will depart from Laszlo in forty-five minutes Universal Time. Please adjust chronometers. In thirty seconds we will have a Universal Time Signal. . . ."

Gildoran automatically checked his chronometer to the small repeated clicks and beeps of the signal.

When it had finished, Rae continued, "*Gypsy Moth* will depart from Laszlo in exactly thirty-eight minutes and twenty seconds. All shipboard visitors must now depart from the Ship. All crew personnel to Departure Stations, please. Intership hookup, Morgan, please."

Morgan—a Class B Laszlan, said, "You have it, Captain."

Gildoran looked round the bridge, occupied with four crew from *Gypsy Moth*, three from *Spray*, and six Laszlans. It was strange to see dark hair, pigmented skins on a bridge within a few minutes of takeoff. Gilrae was taking reports from Nursery, asking about the condition of the twelve Laszlan babies snuggled down there under the care of the Poohbears.

Gilrae put aside her Communicator and said "You three had better get to Departure Stations." She stood up and briefly embraced Gilmerritt. She said, "I won't see you for a while, Merritt; by the time I come off-shift you'll be in the tank, I suppose."

Merritt nodded. "I offered to stay and supervise the medics. But five of the Laszlan Class B people are DNA technicians and surgeons, so they don't need me." She kissed the older woman's cheek. "See you next year, wherever—and whenever—we are then."

Glancing briefly at Gilrae for permission, Gilmarina left her console and came to fling herself into Gilmerritt's arms. She said "Good luck, darling. I know perfectly well if it hadn't been for you I'd be worse off—Gilban said my foot was worse than your hand. If I could have taken your place, I'd have done it, to give you a chance. . . ."

Gildoran asked "Do you need me on the bridge, Rae?"

"No indeed. Cosmos! It's such a relief not to be short-handed," Rae said. "Take Merritt down and tuck her in, if you want to."

On their way down to the Medic deck, Gildran said "It seems strange to see people who don't *look* like Explorers on the bridge."

Merritt smiled faintly. "Give them four years in deep

space," she said. "They'll be as pale as we are. Anyway, it shouldn't bother us to have the babies with dark hair and skins, and if there's an occasional volunteer who doesn't bleach all the way, I think we'll get used to it. It might even be a pleasant variety. Didn't Rae say that homogeneity was the beginning of decadence? Even the Explorers could become decadent, I suppose, if things went too well for too long."

"That'll be the day!" He said "What will we do without Rae, if she keeps her threat to turn Floater?"

Gilmerritt smiled again. "That'll be a long time yet," she said, "Rae *is* the spirit of the *Gypsy Moth* for all of us, and I think she knows it. And by the time she really *does* leave us and turn Floater—well, then it will be someone else. Maybe you." She slipped her good hand through his arm, as they entered the Medic quarters.

Gilban was waiting for them, while the Laszlan apprentice Medics put things in order. Helping to supervise them, Gildoran saw the familiar slender figure, pale smooth hair, strange tilted eyes.

"Ramie, this is a new assignment for you," Gildoran said.

"I wanted a change," Ramie said. "So I'll be taking care of you, Merritt. Are you all ready?"

"In a few minutes." Without self-consciousness, Gilmerritt began stripping off her clothing, ready for the regrowth tank. Ramie picked up a razor and sheared off Gilmerritt's heavy hair. "Easier to look after you," she said, "and by the time you're ready to come out, it'll have grown again."

Gilmerritt lowered her eyes. She said, "Don't look at me, Gildoran."

Gildoran took the woman into his arms. "Don't be a fool, my love," he said. "Do you think I care what you look like, after all these years? Hurry and get well, darling." He picked up the ugly clawed deformity of her hand, stroked it gently and laid his lips to it.

Cosmos! I'll miss her so. . . .

She clung to him for a moment and said "Don't be lonely. It's not fair. You know I won't know or feel anything. Don't you dare miss me when I can't miss you." She reached for Ramie's hand, looking up at her seriously with her great green eyes, and said with strong emphasis, "Ramie. Don't let Gildoran miss me. Or be lonely. Promise."

Ramie kissed Gilmerritt quickly on the forehead and said "I promise. I'll take good care of him, too."

Merritt lay back on the shelf; Ramie covered her with a sheet and Gildoran held her hand while the first of the needles went into her wrist, the one which would put her into the preliminary sleep while her temperature was lowered to hibernation level. Later the useless hand would be amputated and the wrist placed into the regrowth solution, so that a year from now, she would emerge from the tank with only a sense of long dreams—and a hand identical to the one she had been born with.

The internship hookup announced, in Rae's voice, "*Gypsy Moth* will depart the planet in exactly four minutes and eighteen seconds. Stand by for thirty-second countdown. Four minutes. . . . three minutes and thirty seconds . . ."

A preliminary roar of sound, interspersed with bursts of static, began to shake the *Gypsy Moth,* and the floors and walls around them began to tremble. Ramie said "We'd better strap down, Doran."

Everyone else on the Medic deck was already fastened into takeoff seats. The two Explorers went to adjoining seats and fastened the takeoff harnesses around waist and shoulders. Through the growing noise of the takeoff and the drives coming into action, Gildoran kept hearing Merritt's parting words. "Ramie. Don't let Gildoran miss me. Or be lonely. Promise." And Ramie had promised.

Gildoran reached out his hand between the seats and felt Ramie's slender fingers close over his own. Yes, they belonged together. Merritt knew that, too. He didn't know how it would work out. It wouldn't be the same kind of relationship he had with Merritt. It didn't matter. Whatever it was, it would be the right thing for the two of them.

"Thirty seconds. . . . twenty . . . ten. . . . seven, six, five. . . ."

With a shuddering, a scream and a glorious roar, the *Gypsy Moth* lifted from the surface of her homeworld, on another stretch of her endless voyage into Cosmos.

FRITZ LEIBER

062190	The Big Time	95c
791525	Swords Against Death	$1.25
791723	Swords and Deviltry	$1.25
791624	Swords Against Wizardry	$1.25
791822	Swords in the Mist	$1.25
792226	The Swords of Lankhmar	$1.25
951467	You're All Alone	95c

Available wherever paperbacks are sold or use this coupon.

A AT THE EARTH'S CORE

B BACK TO THE STONE AGE

FRAZETTA POSTERS!
SEE NEXT PAGE FOR DETAILS

C THE OAKDALE AFFAIR

D SAVAGE PELLUCIDAR

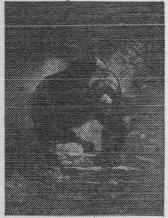

FIRST TIME EVER
BY POPULAR DEMAND

ORIGINAL 4-COLOR
FRANK FRAZETTA POSTERS FROM ACE'S CLASSIC
EDGAR RICE BURROUGHS SERIES

ONLY $3.00 EACH
75¢ handling for each group of 1-4 posters

TOP QUALITY PAPER APPROXIMATELY 18" x 24"

A   B   C   D

PLEASE SEND ME THE FRAZETTA POSTERS CHECKED BELOW

A_____ B_____ C_____ D_____

CHECK OR MONEY ORDER ENCLOSED FOR $_____
(SORRY, NO COD'S. PLEASE—NO CASH)

☐ PLEASE NOTIFY ME WHEN NEXT
   4 FRAZETTA POSTERS WILL BE AVAILABLE

Ace Books, (Dept. MM) Box 576, Times Square Station
New York, N.Y. 10036

Name_____

Address_____

City_____ State_____ Zip_____